Contents

Dedication

For Jim

Thanks for all your patience and not throwing me out along with the laptop.

For all my family and everyone who knew and loved Alice.

Disclaimer

This is a work of fiction based on the journal and recollections of Alice. With the exception of Alice, her husband and children, all other names and characters are works of fiction. I have taken historical information and woven her story around the events and her memories of the time.

Prologue
January 28th 1986

The rocket broke free from its gravitational hold, lifted high into the azure sky, the space shuttle riding piggy back on the huge rocket. Down below on terra firma, thousands of spectators looked to the skies. The crowds were shielding their eyes. The day was clear and the glow from the rocket burn was fiercely bright. All eyes were skyward, glad to be witnessing this momentous occasion. Flags were waved and smiles were seen. The column of white light lifted the coupled space vehicles. The spectators followed the trajectory, craning their necks, marvelling at the technology that could free them from the pull of the Earth. They were in awe of such a spectacle.

Seventy three seconds in, they watched in horror as the explosion showered the sky with debris, the white force still propelled the remnants upwards and then sent two opposing plumes east and west in a huge Y shape. Falling debris criss-crossed the sky.

The couple sitting in their arm chairs looked at each other and continued to watch in silence. The images were self-evident. It didn't need a commentator. The picture switched to the control room, heads in hands, shock and then the image of the falling debris, a white plume spiralling back to earth and the sinister trail of the Y. They knew this was the end of the space shuttle Challenger. They had seen the picture of the seven crew, two of which were women.

They continued to watch in shocked silence, it was nothing new, they always watched in silence.

Joe got up to make a cup of tea, walking heavily and coughing. He was finding it harder to breathe easily. He suffered with emphysema; the chemical industry had not helped with his ailment. He was glad to be retired, but he was in ill health and sad. What he had witnessed seemed to permeate his being and although his wife had said how sad it was and had looked very shocked; she still had a meal to prepare and life to go on with. Joe just felt heavy and tired.

Joe watched his wife as he sat astride the chair; he always sat the wrong way round with his chest resting on the chair back, arms folded on top. This he felt enabled him to grip the chair and open up his rib cage, he felt more comfortable that way. He watched his wife at the window of the kitchen. She smoked her cigarette and pushed the slats of the venetian blind downward to open the window. He pulled up the zip on his cardigan. She wasn't aware he had sat there. He continued to look at the back of her head and watched as the smoke wreathed her blonde hair. He knew it was from a bottle, but it still looked good on her. She had been and still was a very handsome woman and always smartly dressed. She turned and jumped as she saw him there and smiled. She flicked her ash into a little brass ashtray fashioned like a slipper and asked him if he wanted another cup of tea.

Did she know how sad and deflated he felt, did she realise how ill he was? He didn't know. He only knew that he loved her and wanted her to be happy and above all he wanted people to know about her, to understand that her life had been very hard. People needed to know that.

He returned to the living room and eased himself into the brown striped chair and reached to the King Charles spaniel by his side. He laughed to himself that his wife had wanted to call the dog Bryan. Bryan was the name of a young man, a friend of his son and daughter in law. He had driven them to the kennels and they had returned with the puppy nestled on his wife's lap in the back of his Ford Granada. It took some time to gently suggest that they call the dog with its long kennel club name... Rusty. Just Rusty. It was enough. The dog was silky and warm as it lay across his master's feet. "You be a good dog" he said to it, "You look after Alice"

It was later that evening that his younger son popped in.

Joe made up his mind. "Take me to the hospital son, my chest isn't too good" He patted the dog and then kissed his wife; she said she would see him later. As he left the house, he knew. "Goodbye Alice" he thought to himself, "I hope they will be kind to you and I hope they will understand just how remarkable you are"

Anon to sudden silence won,
In fancy they pursue
The dream-child moving through a land
Of wonders wild and new
In friendly chat with bird or beast
And half believe it true
Alice! A childish story take
And with a gentle hand,
Lay it where childhood's dreams are twined
In memory's mystic band,
Like Pilgrim's withered wreath of flowers
Plucked in a far-off land.

From Alice's Adventures in Wonderland by Lewis Carol.

A ninety three year old woman sat beneath a tree, basking in the sun of late September; she was sitting in the garden in a place called Pibrac, in the area of Toulouse, South West France. She was amazed as she watched red squirrels and also saw lizards basking on the warm stones. It was her birthday and she started to reflect again on her life. Write it down, she was urged; write it down, so she set down her memoirs in a little purple notebook. This is a novel based on her recollections hereafter indicated in italics. All family names and characters have been altered and created by the author.

Chapter 1 Ireland 1920

So this was what would be called a soft day. When she had looked out of the window ten minutes earlier she had not seen the rain, but standing there by the garden gate; she felt the damp drizzle on her skin. The drops of moisture collected on her fair eyelashes and she knew her hair would become a frizz. Mama would not be at all pleased as it had been ragged last night and it should be falling in tight little rolls that bounced as she walked. The blue ribbons were already plastered to her cheeks. She should go back into the house, but she continued to stand at the wooden gate flanked by the dry stone wall, with its hollyhocks and delphiniums and climbing roses that wandered at will all over the crumbling stone.

She had seen the two men across the way, heads low together their flat caps almost touching and they had a way of looking around, watching and nervous. She thought that they were like the greyhounds that her uncle bred, ready to run, all edgy and jumpy. The men were watching her too and she dared to look back at them. Alice wondered why they bothered to whisper, it made no odds to her. Mama had talked about people being shifty and she felt that this was what they were being. They were getting wet too, with their grey shirt sleeves rolled up and their bare arms glistening. They were trying desperately to light a cigarette and cupped their hands around the spark of the match and the tall one with the sandy coloured hair drew heavily on the cigarette, once he had it lit. He blew the smoke up into the rain filled sky. Alice watching, thought it was an odd thing that grown-ups did, but she liked the smell of her father`s pipe tobacco. It seemed a more proper thing to do, what gentlemen like Papa would do. When he came into the parlour in the evenings he would sit her on his knee and usually he was still wearing his dark green uniform and she loved to chink the shiny black buttons together and feel them smooth in her hands. She cast her head down and kicked up a few small stones. She was still trying to remember, Papa`s buttons, stones on stones, the strike of a match, the song he sang about a chick, chick, chicken. His voice was less clear now and Mama`s too, she must try to keep from forgetting.

The two men were looking straight at her now and they were talking about her for sure. These were just farm hands and no doubt if Papa saw them there he would shout at them to get back to work, so she wasn`t really afraid of them; but never the less they made her feel uncomfortable.

One waved his hand at her and seemed to be indicating the house, the other put his forefingers into the corners of his mouth and stretching his cheeks wide he put out his tongue and waggled it at her and when he could no longer maintain this, he made circular movements close to his head in a fashion indicating that she was crazy. Nothing new there, some of her brothers and sisters did the same. Not the older ones, no, they were kinder, besides, some of them were married with children of their own. Alice was the youngest of sixteen. This was a large Catholic family in this little village in the soft greenery of County Galway. There were fourteen now as James had died last year, he had been three and often Alice was left to look after him, so when he died so suddenly with the fever and the rash, she was devastated and now she was the youngest. What had happened to Maeve? Alice went to school and then one day when she came home, Maeve was gone and no-one spoke of her. Alice tried asking her parents, but they just said she was away. The whispering had started then.

Her Mother was coming up the path, feet crunching on the gravel, she still called out, it was habit. She caught Alice by the shoulder and spun her around, the startled girl looking at the mouth that moved and knew her mother was cross. In six months the world had changed for Alice, seeing the frightened face Aileen was suddenly back there again, her poor child in that hospital. How could it be she behaved like this, conforming to old habits? She knew that her child was deaf, she could never forget that, but still she was calling out to her.

As a toddler, Alice had been the one with the permanent running nose, the endless coughs and the bouts of earache that made her cry so hard that she kept her brothers and sisters awake. In later years her mother had had to move Sean into the room with Bridie and Bernadette as he was being woken up with Alice`s crying. "Mama, you need to take Alice to see the doctor" Bridie wailed "I can`t stand being woken every night,

"It`s not fair, it really is not!" Mary was softer and more considerate of her little sister. "Maybe she`s in a lot of pain, you need to ask her Mama?"

Aileen felt that her parental responsibilities were being questioned, but later that day when Alice was sitting looking at a book but holding her hand to her head she called to her and the little girl willingly went to her mother. "Do your ears hurt you so; do you still have the pain in your throat?" With tears in her eyes she nodded her head and confirmed that this was the case. "Open your mouth wide now and let me see" she was not a physician, but when she looked in her mouth and saw the redness at the back of her throat, she knew it was a painful thing. "Let me take a look at your ears and all, oh my goodness Alice--- I didn`t know about this" A yellowish discharge was trickling from her left ear and Alice started to whimper. "No school tomorrow my girl, we must take you to see Doctor O`Brien"

Bridie was somewhat pleased that maybe now she would get some peace, but still did nothing to say she was sorry for her sister's pain. She did feel sorry a bit, but not enough to say so. When the doctor looked into Alice`s throat he could see immediately the white swollen nodules of her tonsils and the red raw throat. Her ears were also badly infected.

 "Mrs. Regan, Alice is suffering a great deal here, poor wee mite--- I think we should consider these tonsils coming out and maybe then the ears will become less infected, in the meantime I will give her something for the pain. I will arrange for you to see a senior doctor in Dublin"

"Will I go to hospital Mama?"

"Yes"

"Will you be there too?"

"I will take you on the train Alice, it will be an adventure. I will ask Aunt Maggie to come with us."

Aileen had a dread of hospitals and her cousin Maggie was the right person to accompany her as she was always so confident and kind too.

When the time came to go to the hospital, the children were told to gather in the yard and her father came to gather her up and kiss her.

"Be brave little chicken, we will come and see you soon when it is time for visitors. Don`t be making any fuss now, be a good girl"

She clung to her father, arms around his waist and he gently prised her arms from him and she climbed into the pony and trap that would take her and her mother to the station. Normally the thought of a train ride was exciting, not something they did often but she had gone once with her big sister and her family to the coast. She had loved the smell of the smoke and the sound of the wheels as they clackety, clacked over the rails. Now she listened to the pony`s hooves and the wheels as they turned on their way to the station and felt her heart beating wildly. The countryside flashed by in all its greenery and Alice gazed on the scene. Half way to Dublin the train pulled into a little station and they had to alight and cross over the platform to change trains. Alice was round eyed and beginning to enjoy the adventure but it suddenly became very frightening as her Aunt Maggie pulled her roughly into a waiting room.

"What are you doing Maggie?" Her Mama demanded and also cross that she was man-handling Alice.

"Sh!" she replied fingers to her lips and pointed to the soldiers marching up and down on the platform.

"Be careful Alice or the English soldiers will shoot you!"

"Maggie don't be talking so and frightening the child, you are over-reacting!" Alice could tell her Mama was cross and besides the soldiers just seemed busy marching up and down. Fortunately there was no time to carry on the conversation as their train roared in whistling blowing smoke, steam and smuts. Settling in to their carriage, Alice felt that Aunt Maggie and her Mama were not happy with each other.

Arriving in Dublin was like flying to the moon, so different to rural Kiltormer. The pavements full of people and the general noise and business was so alien. Her mother had to pull her past the shop windows on O'Connell street. Aileen shuddered and noticed the scars on some of the buildings, reminders of the six days of violence four years ago at Easter. She involuntary tugged even harder at Alice. The world seemed so full of violence, had she herself not seen the ragged men returning home after the Great War.

"Mama look at the toys, look!" Aileen was about to march onwards when she suddenly realised again the ordeal her daughter was about to endure. She needed to keep calm for her child's sake, she needed to focus on her needs. She also wanted to show Maggie that she was in charge now and she didn't appreciate her scare mongering.

"Alice go and look, let's see if there isn't a nice new dolly for you"

Her blue eyes lit up. "Oh please Mama--- thank you!"

In the shop were dolls with their china faces and their real hair in plaits and ribbons. Their soft kid bodies were wearing the finest dresses Alice had ever seen. They were the sort of dresses she would have loved to wear too. Although the farm did fairly well and her father's wages were not to be sniffed at, clothing all the children often meant they wore hand me downs. She chose a doll with ruby red lips and dark black hair; she had dark red ribbons in her plaits. "Peggy" said Alice "My doll Peggy" and she hugged her to herself.

"Why Peggy?" Asked her mother

"She is a girl in my book"

Alice and books. Books and Alice, she would be happy in a corner somewhere lost in the printed words.

Aileen was hot and bothered, glad that she had given Alice the time to choose the doll; but now she was afraid that they would be late for their appointment. The little girl's strides were not as long as hers and she was fairly dragging the child along. "Get along Alice, please, for the love of God, will you not move yourself"

"Sorry Mama, I am trying to go faster"

Aileen soon realised that in this large city, she was becoming hopelessly disorientated, she rifled in her bag with all of Alice`s things and found the letter with the address. An elderly gentleman was coming up the road with the River Liffey shining behind him. The man covered his eyes and squinted at the paper. "----The Royal Victoria--- can you tell me how to get there?" she was getting slightly panicked. "Ah `tis the Eye and Ear, folk hereabouts do call it such—ah the Eye and Ear be a fair walk for little feet--- best take the tram---- for you ladies and the girl look fair beat" It was a welcome ride and Alice could look around more leisurely and try not to think too much about the hospital. She already knew that Mama expected her to be brave. Her mother was also taking in the sights and sounds of Dublin. There were many horse drawn vehicles on the road and the sounds of hawkers peddling their wares, she noted too the new shorter hairstyles of some of the women; almost masculine. After the war it seemed that people were trying to start again with new ideas. She thought too that it took money to afford these changes as she watched a woman strolling along the pavement, a fur stole around her shoulders and her figure hugging dress just skimming her lower calves revealing her ankles and shoes with the new heel. Aileen also noted the flat busted look that some of these women had adopted. Alice sensed her Mother`s disapproval, as Aileen tutted under her breath.

Soon the hospital was looming grandly in front of the anxious little girl. She thought it was surely the largest building she had ever seen and a sense of foreboding came over her. It had also come over Aileen but she gripped her daughter`s hand in hers. She held both her white cotton gloves in the other hand; she had removed them as her palms were quite moist. Dry mouthed, the three of them entered the building together.

It was cool in the entrance hall and they both noted the sound of feet clip clopping on the marble floors. White, everything was painted white with chocolate brown woodwork, Alice was craning her neck upwards at the vast staircase, still clutching her doll. The nurses were dressed a bit like the nuns that came to visit school sometimes. Alice and her friends had joked about them moving around on small wheels. She was too nervous to smile now. They were shown the way up the two flights of steps and into the small waiting area. The first thing Alice noted was the lingering odour of cabbage mixed with the general hospital smell; she wrinkled her nose and tried not to wear a face of disgust.

Alice was told to remove her pretty corn-flower blue dress, and she was made to wear a dark blue cotton gown. Her mother was showing disgust now, because it was too large and swamped the child making her look like something from the work house. All too soon it was time for her to leave her Mama and Aunt Maggie and the tear streaked face was turned up

11

toward her mother. "Now Alice, you be good, no causing trouble, I will stay here with your Aunt Maggie and I will be here when it is all over, do you understand" Alice nodded and took her mother's handkerchief. "No tears!" It was a command, so she held them back best as she could and then she seemed to float out of the waiting area with the nurse holding her hand and telling her not to look back. It was common practice for the tonsils to be removed as a day case, so there was nothing Aileen or Maggie could do but wait.

The doctor who came to see Alice that afternoon was tall and abrupt and had a very gruff voice. He lowered himself over her bed and looked into her ears and put the small wooden stick into her mouth and made her say "Aah!" He declared to his entourage, that her tonsils were indeed very infected and puss filled. "Leetle girl---- you `ave very sore throat no?--- We sort this for yoo--- all go today—Ok?" She wondered what the funny smell was each time he lent over her. She was cowering on the bed.

A small white cap was placed on her head tucking in all her blonde hair and they placed the black rubber mask over her face. The smell of that rubber and the ether, were smells that she would be able to remember until her dying day. Alice was terrified and struggled as she succumbed to the ether and then the procedure started. This Italian surgeon was getting used to living in colder climes, but he had been fighting the stress of work and private stresses from his marriage difficulties, so he often felt the need of something to steady his nerves. His nursing staff noted this today as the familiar odour was on his breath and each wondering if they should call a halt to this procedure. They each were afraid of the implications for themselves. Half way through the procedure, to everyone's amazement and to Alice's terror; she opened her eyes and seeing all the faces and the bloodied knife in his hand, she screamed. In the panic that ensued the writhing girl was placed under the mask again and chloroform given, but as the procedure continued it was also noted that the surgeon's hands shook and he perspired profusely.

When Aileen reached Alice, she found a child screaming in terror pointing to her ears and saying over and over "I can't hear, I can't hear!" Her skin was ghastly pale with a grey pallor and her breathing was very laboured. She was also very sick and bringing up copious amounts of blood. "This is to be expected" Aileen was told. Furious she demanded to know what had gone on. There was no satisfactory explanation.

Aileen could only imagine what it had been like for Alice in that hospital without her mother, no one to hold her hand but that was procedure and now they were all aware that she could hear nothing. She did not know how terrified her daughter was, how Alice watched the distorted features of the medical staff, who were equally panicked, mouthing at her; unable to discern what they were saying. Liam had taken a day to travel to Dublin to ask again and again, what had gone wrong? The doctor who had performed the procedure explained that they had been informed that the removal of tonsils was still a relatively new procedure and in all medical procedures there are always risks. So was the deafness permanent? Nobody could predict this, they talked about it all being a waiting game. They would assess her in six months. Liam had been approached by one of the nurses who told him that she was putting her career on the line and said she felt sure the doctor had been drinking. It was not the first time apparently, but this could not be corroborated. There was no question of them being able to bring a complaint against a senior hospital doctor, after all her husband was only a Police sergeant from a remote country village and despite all of his rank and standing in the local community it held no sway in this incident. The senior doctor was an eminent figure in the "Eye and Ear" and nothing they could say would be taken seriously or change what had happened to their daughter. It was an unfortunate event that had to be accepted. So Alice had entered her silent world.

Chapter 2

Aileen was angry, angry for all the hurt, her frustrations, her daughter`s disability, angry with the rain; angry for the fact that she was late in preparing the meal for Father O`Connell. She turned and waved her arms at the farm labourers and she told them to get about their business. The sandy haired one extinguished the cigarette, crushing it beneath the heavy work boots. As he did so he looked at the pair with such malice and to Alice it felt as if she too was being crushed. She gazed on the pair over her shoulder as her mother hauled her up the path and into the parlour.

The parlour was a hive of activity as Tom and Jack the ten year old twins set the table with Mama`s best white crockery and the raven haired Bernadette aged eleven, placed the silver cutlery with the family monogram, on the clean linen table cloth. Alice was ordered to move the big brown pottery jug full of pink roses and set it on the walnut table just inside the front door. Bridie, aged fourteen, with the same blonde hair and blue eyes as Alice, helped her mother strain the vegetables. Mary, twelve and Sean eight were placing glasses and a jug of water on the table to compliment the setting. Alice watched the door open and in came her father, a tall man with his greying hair and large bristling moustache, his whole demeanour commanded respect and he got it. He was the local sergeant in the Royal Irish Constabulary. The children came to him and he ruffled their hair or kissed the girls on the top of their heads, he cuffed Sean on his head for having a dirty face; but with Alice he held her up in his arms and close to her face he mouthed."Hello little chicken" Bernadette pulled a face at Alice behind her father`s back and put her hands over her ears. Alice knew she was mouthing the word "deafy!" "deafy!"

Father O`Connell came to tea, it was for him that the finery was laid out and Mama seemed to be entertaining as if he were the Holy Father himself. She was stiff and cross and not so tolerant of the normal shenanigans. She was not a soft touch, no; but she was not normally so stiff. Father O`Connell said Grace and asked the children questions about their day and each felt that he might ask them about their catechism, but not today. He smiled genially at Alice but made no attempt to question her. The potatoes were passed and the stew eaten and the family meal was pleasant enough but Mama and Papa seemed edgy.

Brigitte, Bernadette and Mary being older were allowed to sit in the scullery and attend to their schoolwork, whilst Alice, Sean and the twins were sent to their bedroom as lamps had been lit and it was time for prayers and bed.

Each child said goodnight and soon in the dim light of the oil lamp, just the parents and Father O`Connell remained at the table.

"That was a fine meal you provided there, Aileen, 'tis not a lie that your culinary skills are the envy of many a woman round these parts. A warm welcome is always found here."

Aileen blushed and added "No flattery Father, I know you say the same to old Widow O`Shaughnessy, but welcome you are!"

"Liam, Aileen, I know that this year and the last have been difficult times, with your dear James gone before, God rest his soul and the sad business of Maeve---- Aileen 'tis all for the best there—to be sure it is--- and now we need to talk about Alice."

Aileen blanched, for talk of their losses made her feel quite faint. She often wondered what she had done to be meted out such a basin full of troubles. She was what would be considered a handsome woman, not beautiful, nor plain neither, but hers was a bold striking, confident face, with a comportment to match. The fashion of the day with the high necked lace blouse and the long black skirt suited her well. This evening she wore her mother`s cameo at her neck and her brunette hair was piled in a bun and fastened with pins at the nape of her neck. Usually she would not let the girls touch her hair, but lately she had realised that she liked the pleasing sensations that tingled her scalp and spine, the feelings that came when Alice wielded the brush and made her locks shine with a hundred strokes. She told herself that it was for Alice, to make the child feel needed, to draw the child close again. Lately she felt her maternal instincts were waning.

Aileen hadn`t yet confessed to Father O`Connell, that when James was born just over three years ago, she had silently hoped and prayed that he would be her last. She had suffered the endless miscarriages, the hopes, the grief. She had felt her body swell so many times, unable to see her feet, unable to stand with the pain in her lower back. She had suffered nausea and had laboured tirelessly to receive each blessed child. With each of her early pregnancies and the safe delivery of each child her heart had felt full of maternal love and in nursing, her pains had been quickly forgotten; until the next time. There had been losses and joy. When James was born she was already forty two, she felt old, to her, her body was worn out and she longed for rest. Her older sister Bernadette had come from Dublin to assist with the birth. The local midwife had been called and she heaved her large body, up and down the stairs, her breathing laboured like Aileen`s. In the early hours before the rooster crowed, James filled his lungs and bellowed, his entry into the world had been brutal and for his mother, she was spent.

"You have a fine boy, Aileen, will you look at him now. He has Liam`s nose an all. God be praised!" Bernadette was trying to encourage her sister. The midwife however noted that he was a little scrap and that it had taken far too many slaps to get him to take that life-affirming first breath. Aileen silently wept and asked God to end her child bearing days. She later became drenched in sweat, convincing herself that her sinful thoughts would not go unpunished. She tried to be loving; she tried not to have the dark days, when she took to her bed with the dreadful headaches. She tried to be tolerant of a house full of noisy children, but she had been there so many times before and wished like the grandchildren, she could hand James and Sean and the twins to someone else. Mrs. Delaney came to help with the cleaning and the endless laundry, but Aileen was still exhausted. Then three years old, after so many coughs and bouts of pneumonia, the little body of James succumbed to yet another attack. He died. He died in her arms, burning up with fever and limp in her arms long before he drew his last breath. It was in her dark agony that she clung to Liam, afraid that her thoughts would escape her head and if she dared to utter them, he would blame her. Her husband stroked her long hair and kissed her, but he did not have the words of comfort that she longed to hear. The Police sergeant did his duty well, but feelings were something he found hard to express. The truth was, he did feel, he felt that something in him had died too.

"Will you have a drop of the hard stuff father?" Liam was already turning the key in the large walnut cabinet with its glass doors and crystal decanters and glasses that Aileen`s father had had etched with the family crest, the gothic style F, reminding all of the prominence of the Flatterly family. Liam being a police officer, a good catholic and well liked in the village, had made her marriage acceptable in their eyes. Father O`Connell accepted the whisky inhaling it deeply and staring into his glass as if it would provide him with the words he needed to utter. The warmth when it hit his throat made him feel more at ease in his body and he continued.

"I was thinking of Alice, Alice is like a little bird with an injured wing who cannot fly. She was the one I thought might take the faith, the one I thought so near to our Blessed lady. She had an eager mind and learnt so well, she attended to her catechism and was devout with prayers. She has a quiet way with her—"

"Father, please— with respect, the girl is deaf, not dead. As far as I can see she still has a keen mind and—"

"Liam, I am sorry, I was talking of my own sorrows, I was unfeeling forgive me. But how is she to progress with her schooling, here in Kiltormer we have no teacher who can help her? There is no one to understand the girls` strange vocalisations, she in turn cannot understand what Miss Linehan is saying—"

16

"Father, what you say has many truths, but Mary Linehan has told me that our Alice is quick to remember what is written on the board, her arithmetic and spelling are faultless and she has a good imagination and has always written the most creative of stories, it is a matter of time and patience for us all I believe, `tho in truth I know it becomes more difficult day by day,--- don`t please give up on her father—she is still a good girl"

Father O`Connell placed his glass on the table and hauled his large frame around the table and came to stand beside Aileen he took her hands in his and softened his tone.

"My dearest Aileen, dear lady. I know all that troubles you and I pray daily to ask that these troubles pass from you, but we are not at liberty to question what the Good Lord has decided, he gives and he takes away. May he have mercy on the soul of dear Alice, but she cannot remain at the school here. She needs to go where she will receive the guidance of the Church and where there are those who can help the deaf and the dumb. Mary Linehan loves the child so she does, but at what price for the others in the class? As you know ours is a small school and catering for the age range that she does, she has no time for individual teaching. No. There is a good school in Dublin that is experimenting in new techniques for the deaf and it is run by the sister of Father Flynn. I think we should let the Church decide the matter in hand for the education of Alice"

Liam had stood up and was now loading his pipe with tobacco, but at the last words he slammed his fist down hard on the table making the little glass of port that Aileen had been sipping, jump to the floor and shatter. "She is our daughter, she was born into this family, she is a bright girl---- this, this—is just too brutal--- she is still the same child---our darling little girl and I won`t entertain the idea of her being sent away---- hasn`t the Church taken charge too much in this family,----take the subject of Maeve---"

"No Liam please, please don`t disrespect the Father, please don`t bring shame on us by speaking of Maeve--- I--- we—have always kept a clean house--- I can`t talk of Maeve"

"Damn you!" her husband bellowed

"Liam please--- don`t blaspheme and the children will hear you---for pity`s sake don`t bring more shame on this house."

"Well she won`t hear us that`s for sure---no Father we will leave things until the autumn—then if things are no better--- then---then –maybe we will discuss the matter again—but when I say so--- do you hear!

"Liam, apologise to Father O`Connell." Her anguish was tangible and she wrung a small handkerchief in her hand.

The Reverend Father was struggling too; he was always the messenger the one who conveyed the declaration of the church. He questioned many things, he prayed for guidance and often thought that his ideas of God were not the same as that of the others who shared the calling. He thought now of Maeve, he must address the issue.

"Now I have heard tell,---well mostly Mrs. Laird hears, my house keeper --- she has overheard some crones in the stores etc. speculating about Maeve so they are. So what`s to be done what`s to say to all who ask? There are those who think it is that she is with child—so I think we need to say something don`t you?" Aileen worked the linen in her hand wringing it like a wet sheet on wash day. "I know who the gossipers are, I know, with their tongues that could clip a hedge--- tell them she`s dead. Tell them she`s dead--- no one must know she has the consumption--- it would be better if she did have a child---only the poor and the dirty have the c—I can`t even bring myself to say it---she must have caught it from some protestant boy she has been seen with--- ---- haven`t I suffered enough!!" Aileen suddenly pulled herself up short realising that she was not including her husband in their suffering and sniffing and dabbing her eyes, she apologised, but to whom she was not sure.

The matter of Maeve was decided, in truth she was desperately ill in the sanatorium attended by the reverend Mothers, but asking for her own. She did not know that the family said she had gone to teach in America and that her family had not approved of her leaving. She did not know that her younger siblings were puzzled and the older ones sworn to secrecy. All desperately sorry for Maeve, but glad that it was her not them in that awful place. Untruths were sometimes considered the lesser of two evils. Aileen wrestled with her emotions, should she go to see her daughter, could she risk bringing the filthy disease back to the family? Three weeks later when she dressed ready to go to the sanatorium at county Wicklow a long journey, so she had made arrangements with Mrs. Delaney to take care of the children and she would be back maybe in a day or two. She would just go, there was no point in trying to explain away her departure, Liam and she had agreed that the children would be told she had gone to Aunt Kathleen to help with a sick child. Her determined attitude did not alleviate her sense of foreboding. She had just placed a thick veil over her face, her leather bag ready when Father O`Connell entered the kitchen with just his customary rap on the door. He would still be in their lives, even if Liam ranted at him in his anguish. He seemed to know where Aileen might be heading and took her by the arm.

"Oh Aileen" he said, " It's all over, I got word from the Reverend Mother, Maeve passed away this morning. She died with her rosary in her hand and a Hail Mary on her lips---- she had peace at the end---so she did—" and Aileen fell into his arms sobbing.

Liam sat in the parlour staring at his beloved gramophone. "His Masters`
Voice", he said the words to himself and with a maniacal laugh, wanted to
fling the large discs to the floor. His stiffness and reserve were in those
moments broken. He had lost two very dear friends to the Great War, he
had lost his son James, he had lost count of the times he had held Aileen
as yet another child died before its time, he had just lost Maeve and now
this with Alice. Oh dear God, Alice. How could he ever again enjoy the
pleasures of music? To know that his little chicken would not enjoy
laughter, the piano, Old Mac`s accordion and how could they ever go
forward. What future was there for her? She was changing fast. Unable to
hear her own voice she had resorted to a thick vocalisation with
unexpected rise and fall in volume and intonation. To make matters worse
with the impairment had come a disturbance to her balance, so she
regularly stumbled. She could not walk a straight line. It was sad to see
how quickly she had become taunted by those who were once her
playmates and even her own siblings. He had boxed a few ears because of
this, but he could not protect her from everyone. It was also an
embarrassment, to constantly have to explain that she was deaf, because
for some her wild vocal sounds plus her wavering gait; gave some the
impression that the child had suffered some form of mental illness. The
phrase deaf and dumb was cruel. Alice was not dumb, not by a long shot;
she had received many prizes for her continued excellence in English and
Mathematics. She had many books with her name written in a copper plate
hand, congratulating her on her achievements that scholastic year. Would
that still be the case? Aileen was an educated woman, an incredibly
strong woman who had stood beside him in both their private and public
life. She was he reflected an incredible woman, but sometimes she was
harsh with the children and now she seemed so distant from Alice. It was
almost as if she blamed herself for what had befallen the child. The large
grandfather clock chimed the hour and checking his pocket watch he
realised that he had allowed precious time slip by and he needed to speak
with his wife.

It had been hard for them both to relocate, under the regulations he could
not serve in his home county and neither could he live in the county of his
wife`s family, so here they had come as a newly married couple and this
was the house that had come with the job. This was the place that Aileen
had made home. He was aware how hard his news was going to be. They
were well known in the village and for the most part well liked, but as police
Sergeant; Liam was aware that his duties did not sit well with everyone.

He called to Aileen and she came and sat beside him, noticing the lines
etched into his face and that there was more silver grey in his hair and his
moustache. He had noticed that she too carried more fatigue in her looks
and demeanour. He sighed as he reached for her hand.

"My dear I have had word from Dublin Castle, I have been ordered to relocate to Kylemore barracks. There is a large house there for us and farm land too, but there has been unrest there and --- well,-- it is there that we have to go. I am sorry that we are having to go with all that has passed, but I have no choice in the matter." He looked down at his hands and twisted his wedding ring, he hesitated to look up and see the hurt in her eyes. He knew she was no fool, but he did not want to tell her of the killing of two RIC men in County Tipperary and that the supporters of Michael Collins were growing in numbers, some barracks had already been abandoned and some officers had decided to leave and switch their allegiance, how they had come to that decision he did not wish to dwell on. He only knew that his orders must be obeyed and he was still proud to be an officer in the Royal Irish Constabulary. Aileen felt again that she had no control of her life and that she was just a leaf on the breeze, that she would be blown this way and that and that maybe she would find rest someday. Maybe Kylemore, would be a better place, how could she do anything other than commence the packing up of their possessions. All the arrangements for their move had already been put in place, it was not sure if any new occupants would inhabit the house she now called home. This was in the hands of those disembodied personnel at Dublin castle.

"Tell the children that it will be a bigger grander house and I will tell Jimmy and his friend Connor that they can come and work on the land, there are wheat fields and stables with horses for the officers. There will be more officers to come into contact with, but there will be no more for you to do,--- Aileen you know that I am grateful for all that you do, I cannot do this alone my dear" He took her hands in his and kissed them. He hoped that she had not noticed the glistening in his eyes.

Jimmy was their eldest son with his wife and they had been working on their present farm, so both hoped that they would be happy to take the new work offered to them.

"So when do we have to go?"

"As soon as possible" he replied and the two sat and held each other as they listened to the steady rhythm of the pendulum in the grandfather clock. It had always felt solid and reassuring like the heart beat of the house. Neither said anything but it felt that this heart was breaking.

Chapter 3

Alice was something of an oddity to her siblings, the older ones were trying their hardest to be patient and to help her, the youngest ones found delight in getting her to read to them and then laugh at her strange pronunciations. She in turn had become quite stoic, she quickly realised that this might be a permanent arrangement, but she hoped that things could be done to give her back some hearing. Some of her parents friends were asking questions and always in front of her, as if she wasn`t there. It was bad mannered of them she thought. She couldn`t hear them but she could sense what they were asking."Are you sure she`s really totally deaf, can she hear this" and would rap on the table or clap their hands together. Some of her younger siblings would peek around the doorframe and snigger at this; her Father would scowl and send them away. "I`m not blind" Alice would say to herself. Her Mother would then explain that No, Alice could feel vibrations, and was learning to lip read, but could not hear anything at all. Nothing. Alice would then remove herself from the room and go out into the garden or to her room to read books. She had always loved animals and nature and she found that she didn`t need her ears to still be able to appreciate the ants scurrying from their nests with their eggs, whenever she poked the nest with a stick. She loved poking in little ponds and watching spiders spin their webs, thinking her sisters stupid to be afraid of them. The tabby cat had kittens in the barn and Alice often went into the warmth and comfort of the barn, to sit on the hay bales and play with the softly mewing bundle. She told herself that the cat says miaow and the dog barks, the cow says moo and the cockerel says cock a doodle doo, the sheep says baa and the pig grunts. In her mind she could still remember the sounds, but as time went by it became harder to remember exactly. If she closed her eyes tight she would think of Mama`s face and Papa too and then will herself to remember their voices. She hoped she would remember forever, she wished she could hear her own voice to understand why it caused such hilarity with some. Her best friend Aggie still came and played and she did try, but Alice could see their friendship was different now. So often she lagged along behind her older sisters on the way home from school, dawdling; looking into hedgerows and spotting birds' nests and she loved the trickle of water running over her hands as she plunged them into the little stream. She was totally immersed in her own world.

A few weeks before the move to Kylemore, Aileen told Alice that they had to go back to Dublin to see the doctor again. Alice shuddered. She was more and more able to lip read her teacher but with her mother it was harder, she spoke too fast and seemed embarrassed to make the shapes needed in order to lip read and with Papa, his moustache got in the way. So almost everything was written down and Alice could sense her mother`s frustration at having to find paper and pencil all the time. She resented using her pen and ink. She had thrust the note at Alice. It read. "We have to go back to Dublin, you have to see the doctor we are going tomorrow" She must have seen the look of dread and the down turned face and she grabbed her daughter buy the arm and spoke firmly and Alice got the sentiment."Don`t be making a fuss now, I have so much to do, I don`t want to go either, but we have to, so there now don`t be a baby" She rocked her arms to emphasise the bit about being a baby. Alice understood that she was a nuisance. She was sure that her Mother loved her and Papa too, but she understood that she was an extra worry for them and hoped that if she was especially brave the doctor would tell her ears were going to get better.

This time it was just Alice and her mother who made the journey. It was so sad to see the train but not hear it, to watch in silence as the smoke bellowed, to feel the rush of air and see and smell the smuts. She sat in the carriage next to her mother gazing out of the window. "The cow goes moo" she said to herself as she kicked her feet against the underside of the seat and watched fields of cattle flash past. She could feel the train move over the tracks, but there was no comforting clackety clack. If her mother realised the loss of those sounds, she said nothing and continually brushed the hem of her coat with her gloved hands. She glared at Alice as she placed her hands on her legs to stop her kicking. Alice presumed it was too noisy, but she had enjoyed the rhythm trying to emulate the clackety clack.

In the hospital the doctor was waiting in his office. He would not allow Alice`s mother into the room although Alice had shrilly demanded her mother`s presence. Her cross face showed her disapproval as the doctor`s assistant had to prise her away from her mother. It was the same doctor. The funny smell was different, it smelt like cough drops and he wiped his nose a lot and blew silently into a handkerchief. He also mopped his brow a lot too. His red face leered into Alice`s. He indicated that she should open her mouth, shouting at her when she didn`t understand. He became very agitated and she knew when people were angry. He pointed to her ears and shook his head. She thought he was saying "you are deaf" and as she was taking in her disappointment he reached forward and slapped her face and shouted again. It was just her and him in the room. He wrote on a paper and thrust it in front of her. "YOU ARE NOT DEAF, YOU ARE JUST PRETENDING, TO MAKE TROUBLE FOR ME" Alice screamed and screamed and he hastily screwed up the paper and threw it in the bin. He made it quite clear that she should be quiet. When he led her out to see her mother, he was all smiles. He said something to her mother and then they left. Alice waited until they were outside and tried to explain to her mother what had happened and asked why her mother hadn`t come in with her. Aileen looked at Alice as her voice rose and became almost hysterical. The poor child was clearly traumatised by the whole experience and now was not the time to tell her that there was nothing that could be done, the doctor had been sorry, but sometimes these things just happen. So another long journey for nothing. She couldn't wait to get home.

When they eventually returned home, Liam had been at the station with the pony and trap, this had at least lifted Alice's spirits. Her father could still make her smile even though he had such a formal manner. Later when Aileen reiterated that she had been told that the deafness was irreversible, Liam promised that he would find a way to send Alice to a specialist in London. He was not usually given to rash promises, but he could not see any way of gaining anything in Dublin.

It didn't take long for the house to become a hive of activity with everyone packing up their belongings ready for the move to Kylemore. On the day everyone who could be called upon arrived bright and early and Mr. Delaney came as well as his wife, she was busy in the kitchen making tea and handing out little cakes that were no sooner baked, than eaten. It was noisy and chaotic. Connor and Jimmy arrived with their horse drawn wagons. The large drays used to hauling timber and hay were ably suited for the job in hand. Alice decided to stay in the barn with the cats; she had taken her doll Peggy with her and a pile of her favourite books. She obviously did not know that there was even more excitement when a petrol driven lorry arrived, sent over from the barracks at Kylemore.

"Will you look at that now," said Jimmy, shaking hands with the young constable who had been assigned to drive it over to them. "Is it a Ford?"

"It is that" came the reply and he started up the engine again, basking in a little glory that came with the novelty of such a machine in their midst. Each time he revved the engine there was a huge squeal of delight and much applause. "Tis a wonder to behold" said Mr. Delaney and he stood looking at it in wonder. "My brother Shamus, over at Waterford Bay, tells me he was seeing one of these new flying machines, magnificent, so it was, so it was" He ruffled the hair of one of the twins but he could never name either being identical in all their ruddy complexion and freckles, so he always addressed them as a single unit, like many other people did. "You know, we live in grand times, grand times, that we do, ah that we do" His wife came out into the yard and broke his reverie with a command to get moving. They didn't forget Alice and soon the whole family were on the move and eventually tired but generally all in good spirits, they were able to see the first glimpse of their new home. They had passed through wooded areas and breathtaking scenery to emerge close to Kylemore Lake with the grand towers of the Castle gleaming white in the sunshine. Liam laughed heartily when Sean pointed towards it and laughingly shouted out "our new home Papa?" "Nothing but the best!" He jauntily replied and everyone appreciated that the stiff Police Sergeant had shared this joke. Mrs. Delaney had told them that the Abbey had recently been taken over by the Benedictine Nuns "D'you know that their place in Ypres was destroyed in the war so it was and they have been looking for a new home, don`t you think it`s grand that they were choosing hereabouts, I think it is lovely to think that they have found such a tranquil place, don`t you think?" There was a consensus of opinion that it was indeed a beautiful area, without doubt the finest in all Ireland.

The hedgerows were a riot of colours with reds and crimsons, dancing fuchsias like little ballet dancers with spindly legs under their tutus, or so the ever observant Alice thought. The first sight of the house, took her breath away, they had rounded a corner and started to drop down into a little pass and there with its back to a little copse was the house, with the barracks and its guard house slightly to the left as they faced it and the two buildings faced out across fields of waving wheat. Liam was up front in the lorry with his wife, he saw the light shining again in her eyes. "At last," he thought, "At last, may we have some peace in our lives, may she be happy here"

Chapter 4

The house was grand. It had a beautiful stone entrance porch with a large oak door and brass knocker. Around the porch were growing ivy and honeysuckle and wisteria was making its way across the face of the house. The scent from the honeysuckle was glorious and bees droned busily over its blossoms. The trouble with moving home is that once packed up, everything has to be done in reverse at the other end, at least with such a large family there were plenty of hands to start all over again. Aileen had renewed energy and enthusiasm and went from room to room deciding where she wanted her precious furniture. Liam had wanted to be rid of his gramophone after Alice had become deaf, but she would never be parted from her beloved piano and he had been so very glad that she had persuaded him not to be rash. So the two items now inhabited the parlour along with the rugs and padded chairs that she would prefer no-one sat on. She busied herself in the kitchen with the range that Mrs. Delaney said she would be honoured to black lead, not a job Aileen would want to tackle, but she could see the attraction of the range. There was a scullery and the parlour, the dining room and five bedrooms. Five bedrooms and each had a little fireplace. They could decide who slept where later. Aileen was positively glowing with the idea of being the grand matriarch.

Liam soon busied himself with getting to know his fellow officers and took Shaun and the twins into the barracks. The men were all fairly tall, slim and business like. The area was spick and span, with little if any comforts. Liam showed the boys the kits hanging ready for action. Attached to the leather belt was a long case housing a baton and a square leather pouch which contained handcuffs. The boy's eyes grew wide as they noticed the sword bayonet. There were also the small rifles. One officer explained these were carbines with a six shot magazine and weighing only six and a half pounds. To the question had they ever used them came the assurance that no-one had and they hoped that they never would. Jimmy and Connor had come to stand in the doorway; the men looked at each other in silence as they heard the assurances. The lightness of the day suddenly grew heavy.

So began their life in Kylemore and in those Summer days with school being out, it was an idyllic time of playing out, discovering the trees to climb, the best places for making small dens. For Alice it was where she continued her love of nature. Jimmy came one day and tapped Alice on her shoulder; he beckoned to her to come into the yard. "Come on, come and see what I have bought" she didn`t understand what he wanted her to see but she knew she could trust Jimmy. He was her big brother and one of the kindest, he had taken to calling her chicken too and she loved him for that. He took her hand and led her into the yard by the barn at the rear of the property. There tied up to the iron gate was a black and white cow. "Take a look Alice, here is Daisy. We`ll have our own milk to drink, what do you think?" Alice just beamed, the cow was wonderful. Not long after that Aileen bought some hens and a rooster from a neighbouring farmer and Alice was so pleased to be given the task of collecting eggs. She loved having that responsibility and wasn`t afraid of the pecking and of course the squawking that her sisters disliked didn`t bother her. She liked the discovery and the warmth of the eggs in her hands and would carry them in a wicker basket to her mother. Mama seemed to be smiling more and less cross these days. One day she beckoned to Alice and told her to come into the barn, she was smiling so Alice knew it had to be something good. "For you, Happy Birthday" there was the cutest, liveliest little puppy. A russet red Irish setter, her uncle bred greyhounds and setters and this pup had been chosen specially for her. He immediately smothered her with his wet tongue and nose, pushing her backwards into the straw and the love affair began. Red as she called him was her constant companion. It was made clear however that no dogs were ever allowed in the house. There were already liver coloured spaniels and a rather portly Labrador that was her fathers, but like them Red would have to live in the outhouse, chained at night. The dog had to be removed from Alice`s bed several times and Alice told off for encouraging it there.

The nights started to draw in and the summer turned to autumn almost overnight there was a chill in the evenings and early morning. School had begun again, but Alice had not joined the local school. Jimmy`s wife Erin was teaching at the local school and had tried to persuade the authorities to let her teach Alice, but it was thought that it would be to the detriment of the other pupils and Erin had no knowledge of how to go about this, but she was willing to learn. The answer was still no. So Alice was enjoying an extended holiday. The fields of wheat had done exceptionally well and were full and golden waving in the breeze and the weather was holding so the talk soon turned to when the harvest would begin. It would mean recruiting extra hands to scythe the crops and then the baling and the storage. Jimmy and Connor sat with Liam one evening and as he lit the gas lamps they talked of the possibility of hiring extra men. "Can we afford to do this, Dada?" "Do you have any objections?" Liam was a little concerned about their wages, but thought that they could hire just for the harvest they had no choice in truth and some of Delaney`s men had asked for work too. "There are the men we hired at Kiltormer, Dada, I hear that they have not been able to find work since we left, do you no think we should consider them?"

Liam left the hiring to his boys. They would know who to trust and besides he had his own duties to attend to. The "Lock-up", as the twins and Sean referred to it hadn`t seen any occupants for a while. There had been a few drunken brawls in the public bar in the village and one man had made off with another man`s wife and that had come to blows too. So they had been "invited" to spend time behind bars in the barracks gaol. There was the poaching and sheep stealing, and the knocking out of a few teeth, but lately it had been a quiet beat. The officers were assigned to walk a twelve mile circuit, twice a day and again at night. It meant being out on the hills and in wooded areas. So the management of the farm was in the hands of Jimmy and Connor. In all some twenty men were available and all of them had been desperate for work. So they came to start the harvest.

Red, was a gangly disobedient dog, lolloping everywhere with his wet warm nose always eager to nuzzle Alice's palm, but try as she might he rarely came when she called or even attempted to walk to heel. He had already pulled her over and skinned her knees; they were still sporting the bright yellow iodine stains. She had been laughed at by the boys as Red had come across the yard with Alice squealing and holding the rope leash. The rope had burned her hands as it was wrenched through her palms by the struggling dog. Her pride was severely dented as she landed backwards on her bottom and the errant dog ran off to find the rabbit or whatever it was he had been chasing. "Up you go now Alice, let's be having you now" Jimmy had helped her up and taken her into the kitchen to soothe her hands and knees. He always upturned her chin with his rough hands but gently looked into her eyes when he spoke. She loved him very much "My big brother" she thought. He gave her a glass of the fresh milk from Daisy and put his fingers to his lips. She knew it meant don't tell Mama. Milk was for mealtimes only and maybe before bed, but wasn't there water at the pump, Mama always said; drink water if they were thirsty. Jimmy had returned to the work, the large chestnut horses had been harnessed to the harvester with its clanking metal blades that scythed through the fields and all hands were working in the warmth of the autumn sun.

Alice had helped distribute the lunch that her mother and Mrs. Delaney had made for the men but soon she was wanting to get off and look for Red. Where could the daft dog have got to? She had looked in the barn and in the yard and looking out at the fields he was not there, he knew that he would never be allowed in the house. She soon found that she was rounding the back of her house and coming past the low stone wall that separated her from the barracks and the "Lock up". It was then that she saw the flopping body of shiny red fur. The dog had been hanging around by the side door of the barracks, hoping for some titbit which occasionally he received from an officer on duty. He had his head down, nose to the ground tail thrashing, but he was in no luck today as he was waved at and told to "get away!" Alice was about to run and get him when she saw something strange. Two of the farm workers had gone up to the lock up and were leaning with their backs against the wall to the side of the barred window. It appeared that they were looking straight out across the fields, but every now and then they turned their head slightly towards that barred window and nodded, as if in response to something coming from within.

Alice froze and ducked down under the wall out of sight of the men, she had recognised them. They were the sandy haired man and his friend who had teased her. When she peeped again they were deep in conversation heads down and moving away now from the lock up and holding a piece of paper and studying it hard and then she saw an officer come from inside the barracks. She thought to herself that he would tell them to move away and to get back to work, but to her amazement he seemed to lower himself to their height and with his eyes darting all around he studied the paper too. Alice was puzzled and stretched her body further along the wall trying to crane her head around to see more, but she dislodged a few crumbling stones and she knew to her dismay that they would make a noise. Red who had been nosing around heard this and barking ran towards her. Alice saw the men look towards her and the two farm hands started towards her angrily, but were held back by the officer who seemed to calm them and said something which led to them staying where they were, but the looks all three gave her were very menacing. What could she do? Papa must know that they were there, they weren`t doing anything wrong, but they didn`t look as if they were nice people and why was the officer talking to them like that? What could she tell anyone? Nothing and it always took so long to make people understand and if she wrote it down, what would she say? "I saw three men talking " as far as she knew that wasn`t yet a crime. They on the other hand were glad that their plans had fallen on deaf ears.

Chapter 5

Aileen was puzzled and frightened and asked once more why her money was no longer good enough in this store. She was standing in the village butcher and had come to buy meat for the Sunday roast, a treat for Liam and the boys as the harvest was almost done. The fields were now brown and stubbly with the short stalks and the hay in bales. It was satisfying to hear that the harvest had been a good one. So now she was feeling as if her feet had been swept from under her as this man with his bloody apron, cleaver in hand; stood firm and repeated " Tis sorry that I am , but I won`t be taking your money no more, times are changing and Ireland can`t be paying heed to your dallying with the English officers up a Dublin Castle--- tis Ireland for the Irish and we don`t need orders from England---- so tell your Sergeant----" but he was interrupted by his errand boy who bravely demanded the he not wave the cleaver in the face of a lady. Several women were in the butcher`s shop, that had almost always spoken with Aileen, but now they looked away. Aileen backed out of the shop, determined to keep her tears in check and leave with some dignity, but when she was nearing the farm house she ran inside and sunk sobbing into her chair in the parlour. When she had composed herself she went to find Liam. "What has changed," she demanded to know, "I thought that we were getting on fine with people here- abouts, what are you not telling me? I need to know Liam, tell me" Her husband`s face was ashen as he heard her recount her ordeal and his fists were clenched as he slowly turned to her. "There are those that would see us gone, Aileen, those as you know, who want nothing to do with the English--- those who see us taking orders from the British Government--- those who feel the Royal Irish ---are not Irish----but simply--- the lap dogs of English masters----- how can we police in the face of such resentment?" Then he stopped as he could see that strong though she was, she was clearly frightened. He had not told her that in recent months his wages had increased in recognition of the hardships that the force was facing. He had been told that many of his fellow officers in barracks throughout Ireland had been assassinated and that in the last three months six hundred men had resigned as the threat to them and their families increased. There was even talk that some officers had turned traitor and joined forces with the aggressors. There were even reports of bloody reprisals; the whole area was a tinder box of savage passions.

 "Where will we get meat now, I will have to take the trap miles away and will our money be taken anywhere for sure? Are we in danger Liam? I think you should tell me" He could only take her hands and tell her not to worry the children and that he would do whatever it took to protect his family. Aileen shivered thinking of the armoury in the barracks.

Aunt Maggie's farm across the fields and through the little copse, had a threshing machine, a marvel, driven by steam and as if by magic it had produced the grain that was trickling through Alice's fingers. Without her hearing, she had increased satisfaction in all things sensory. In the warmth of the grain store she would slip in when Jimmy had come over and taken her with him. With the sun playing on the dust motes and the birds roosting in the rafters it was a place that she loved to be. Some weeks before Father O'Connell had come to see the family, he had paid special attention to Alice this time and she had been pleased that he had taken the trouble to write down his instructions for her and he had brought her a prayer book. He had noted that she read her Bible most attentively and that she had in the past scored high marks in her religious studies. She found it hard to read his cursive script and he had waited patiently to see her smile in response. He had written. "This is for you Alice, because when myself or any priest is giving the sermon, you won't be hearing, but God wants you to pray, read his word. We don't always understand his ways and we just have to accept, so you read and pray Alice—remember your duties to our dear Lord and look around you. Use your eyes because His wonders are all around and I know that you love all things of nature, that is when you see God's love close at hand. He loves you Alice and even when life is tough, He will always be with you, I hope you understand this"   These written words touched her to her very soul and she remembered them forever, the Father who could preach fire and damnation also had his gentler side.

Aileen was trying hard to keep things together for her family; she herself was becoming thinner and sacrificing her share of food. They were far from starving but it was harder and harder to find anyone who would serve them. She had been to the general store to buy material to make the girls some coats, but had been refused again and as she walked out saying "You are not being fair--- we are not here to make trouble" She heard one of the women mutter "Will you listen to her--- what would you expect from a pig—but a grunt!!" Some joined in laughing and some just did as they always did and averted their eyes. Aileen's eyes were smarting again. There was a friend of Aunt Maggie who had brought some red material from Dublin and Aileen and her daughter-in-law Erin sat up into the evenings sewing by the oil lamps to make new coats for Alice, Bridie, Bernadette and Mary. The coats would see them through the coming winter and the girls were so proud of them with the black piping and black buttons. New boots would have to wait. The coats were hanging proudly on pegs just inside the kitchen door. Liam had not noticed them as he came in that evening with a hurricane lamp in his hand. Aileen showed them to him as she hoped he would be pleased with her efforts, but she could see the strain on his face. " Do y'know what I have been told today, Aileen, that so many men are turning away, that those who have returned from the Great war are being sent here to shore up the force--- those who have returned to English shores are being sent here and from Edinburgh too--- what madness---it will only enrage and enflame!" He stroked his hair and greying moustache "I am losing respect here, the men are losing morale!"

One summer night, we were all in bed and we all felt and they heard a loud bang on the door downside. I myself did not hear this. Someone told us to get up and go outside. I had woken up to find all in the room up and dressing. Someone, I don`t remember who told me to get up and get dressed. I had taken off my nightdress because it was a hot night and was only wearing my vest and knickers. I had picked up Mary`s dress by mistake but gave it back to her and for her to throw my clothes over; but she wouldn`t and someone behind her told me to hurry and grabbed my hand. On the way to the kitchen downstairs, I saw my new coat that my Mother had made for me a few days ago, hanging on the peg in the kitchen. I pointed it out to my Mother, but no one stopped to grab it, but hurried me outside. When we were outside, we could see the house was already lit, we could see flames at the top of the house and the house was roaring with red and orange flames. Everything in the house was burning. My mother hurried to get the cow out of the barn. Everyone was running. We ran across the fields to Aunt Maggie`s farm. I had no shoes on because they wouldn`t wait for me to find them. The rough stubble cut my feet because the field had been harvested; the others had their shoes on. We lay in the warm straw in the stables at Aunt Maggie`s, I think my mother lay down beside me and my brothers and sisters. In the morning we went back to see the house. We all saw the house was burnt down, the ashes looked grey. My brother Jimmy lifted me onto his back as I had only my vest and knickers and no shoes. He stopped for me to have a look at the house. Then he took me back to our friend`s house. I saw my father was in their kitchen with the rest of my family, he was wearing his uniform of green, The Royal Irish and it was not smart. He had a sore eye. I understood that they were talking about us having to leave and I could lip read the word danger. My Mama said we would leave friends in danger too. I didn`t understand fully. My Mama told my father that I had no clothes except my vest and knickers, also my Mama told our friends that they could have our cow and that she hadn`t been milked. Someone gave me some clothes and socks and boots and soon after we left to go to Dublin.

It seemed to me not long after we got to Dublin, sometime one afternoon an Aunt I didn't really know, came for me and took me into her neighbour`s house to play with her little girls. When I noticed that none of my brothers and sisters were there or my mother or father I began to cry and started to run across the road crying Mama, Mama. A woman was crossing the road from the other side and my aunt called to her to catch me. She did and brought me back. I cried for a long time. No one told me the reason I was held back. My Aunt tried to tell me that I was to go to a school for deaf *children, but no one had told me before. I thought my mother had abandoned me.*

I don`t remember how long I stayed with that aunt, I don`t think it was long. One day she took me, her daughter and her granddaughter Kathleen in her pram, towards the school where I was going. When we got there I was surprised to see the door was opened by a Nun dressed in the habit of a Dominican Nun. They wear a yellow habit with a black surplice and a black veil. I thought they looked lovely. The Nun who took us in took us to see Mother Superior. She was very nice and so friendly. After Mother Superior, whose name was Mother Imelda, had a chat with my aunt, she took me in. I said goodbye and we had to go in through the chapel to the Deaf Department. There was a service going on, I think it was a confirmation service. I saw a crowd of school girls in beautiful white dresses with veils on their heads. So I walked on to the Department of the Deaf. Sister Imelda told me that the deaf do not talk with their lips, they talk with their fingers. I did not know what to think, I did not know this before I met the girls. They were normal girls but they only used their hands for talking. I soon got friendly with them and glad to see that there were girls like me who were deaf, but I was puzzled that we were not allowed to talk with our mouths. I quickly learnt the sign language and was quite happy there.

Chapter 6

In the cold light of the early morning, no one had spoken. They walked around surveying what was left of their home. The ashes were grey and still smouldering. Aileen normally loved the smell of wood smoke. They all stood in disbelief. Now and again someone would kick the ashes with the toe of a boot and disturb the curled edge of a photograph splintered with glass, they would kick aside the glass but the picture retreated into the ash. The curled pages of books, like the burnt wings of many injured butterflies, lay flapping in the breeze. They wandered aimlessly finding little that was salvageable. The charred blackened spars of the building gave scant testimony that this had once been a proud home. Alice was up on the shoulders of Jimmy, someone had placed a shawl around her, as she shivered in her underclothes. Liam was ragged and defeated; the barracks were razed to the ground. He had placed his hands in the air and then clenching his fists turned and walked away. His wife watched as her husband started walking back across the fields toward the sanctuary they had sought last night. The children knew not to ask anything of him and came close to their mother who took their hands and hugged them to her waist, kissing each head and with the air accentuated by sobs they followed the broken image of their father. In the kitchen the children were fed and sent into the yard to fetch water and tend to their two shire horses that had been pulled whinnying from the stables and were now in the paddock. The regimental horses were gone.

"So, Dada what happened? Where are all your men? We have two who are here, but the others where are they?"

Jimmy was standing with his hand upon the hearth staring at the coppers lined up above the mantle and turning to his father who was seated at the wooden table, he saw his mother`s look of concern. "No Mama, we have to know, what has gone on here?" She was hovering by her husband desperate to know herself, but afraid of knowing and afraid for her family. "Aileen, It`s alright—let me speak" he coughed and in a voice that rasped from the smoke inhalation he continued. "Those two---the ones we hired, they were plotting this, all of the men had been got at,---Y`all have to know---they were so scared---- all of them save Padraic and Kelly---they all went last evening ---fled to the hills they did, all the horses --- gone --and I heard shouts—when I came back from duty and the dogs were straining on their chains and barking and barking---- didn`t you hear them ------and those rogues, they had them----Padraic and Kelly were on the floor, ---- punching them and kicking them they were and it`s when I got this—for I flew in with my fists and Mick Delaney ---he must have sore knuckles---" He stopped to catch his breath, "Where are they now, Dada?" Jimmy asked, running his hands through his tousled blond hair, watching his father grip the table for strength. "We gave them hell, that we did and they turned and ran, with their bloody faces streaming and they turned and told us that we would pay----w—well that we have!"

"What about the guns and things Dada--- did they"

"They`re gone—all gone---I don`t know who has what—but they`re gone" Liam told them how he had searched the outbuildings looking for the two rogues, and saw with horror that the arsenal and bayonets were gone. He told how he and his two fellow officers sat shaking, watching in the darkness to see where they had gone and if they would be back. "Soon after we heard a thump and smelt the kerosene and saw the flames-----" He told of how they had beaten the flames with old blankets and how there had been the attempt to quell the flames with the chain of buckets of water--- this they knew for Jimmy and others had come running across the fields. Someone had unleashed the frightened dogs and seen that the stable roof was alight, the two shire horses were snorting and whinnying and would have destroyed the stable themselves with their frantic kicking. Their rescuers had had to avoid those great hooves. The harvest store was well alight and the roof of the house was smouldering too, they had to abandon the fight to quell the flames and get everyone to safety. They had all joined hands, in a long wide chain and run across the newly harvested fields. Jimmy had scooped Alice up onto his shoulders, for she was running in bare feet and the stubble had cut her feet.

"They`ve done for us--- we are finished!" Liam started to cough again and laid his head on the table. Jimmy had never seen his father with so much raw emotion. The proud Sergeant was no more. Later returning to the ashes to see what else he could salvage, Jimmy found the charred and broken body of Peggy, the doll that Alice loved so much. It was then that Jimmy wept.

In the days that followed, some of Maggie`s friends brought clothes and small donations of food. It was however clear that Liam did not want to talk any further as to what had passed and he made his decision and Aileen knew they had no choice. "My brother has the farm in England and he has said we can stay there until we can find something for ourselves---we have to go Aileen—you know our lives depend on that, I can`t be sure if they will come back and maybe finish us all for good--- we have to go and go soon, --but this is past---we never talk of this outside this family d`you hear me. This is our business and ours alone, no more talk"There were accounts of the fire in the local papers but the family declined to give any comment. Ireland was changing and in two more years Ireland underwent partition and by April of 1922 the Royal Irish Constabulary ceased to exist, replaced by the Civic Guard in the Irish Free State and by the Royal Ulster Constabulary in Northern Ireland.

But in those post fire days Aileen felt that she may not have the strength to rise like a phoenix from the ashes and start again, but something did give her the will to do so, she was angry, angry that her husband had been defeated, angry that their family had nearly encountered tragedy. She simply threw herself into packing up the little that they had and started to make arrangements for their passage to England. So she was packing for her and Liam, Tom and Jack, Bernadette, Bridie, Mary, and Shaun. Jimmy was going to stay and that was going to be hard, he had decided that he would stay, he had his life there and besides Erin was expecting another child and wanted to be near her own Mother, he strongly protested that his roots were in Ireland and that he was staying. She was also leaving behind her existing grandchildren and their families, they felt the same way as Jimmy and with no obvious political affinities they felt that they would be able to continue as they had. But what to do about Alice?

Father O`Connell had come to visit and to offer his help. He had known some families in his time that had suffered much, but this family tested his faith sorely. He stood in the yard with his dark cassock flapping struggling to keep his biretta on his head. Aileen hugged him and wept again as she led him into the kitchen. She knew what he was about to say. "This is the time now Aileen there is no putting this off." It was decided that Alice would go to the school for the Deaf in Dublin, it was a boarding school run by Dominican Nuns and Father O`Connell would organise everything. "Now it is best that you don`t tell her just yet, she has a lot to adjust to, it will be kinder if she goes with her Aunt--- the one you will stay with before your passage to England." He saw her face "Aww Now Aileen it is for the very best—you know it tis" and in her heart she knew that this would be the best thing for Alice and when she had regained her voice and they had settled in England, she would come for her and take her to a new life. Yes it would be for the best, so she wouldn`t say anything to Alice or the other children for the moment. She poured a cup of tea for herself and the Reverend Father, why did they always seem to spend so many moments drinking tea together whenever there was something monumental to deal with. When he got up to leave he pulled out an envelope from inside his cassock and passed it across the table " Don`t open it yet--- and I`ll thank you to just take it without any of your shaking head or protestations----"she had seen the notes protruding from the corner of the envelope---"---Take it Aileen---it is from my Parish---we had a collection and there is some that I added. God be with you, my dear Aileen and I will pray for you and your family for as long as I have breath in my body" She flung her arms around his neck and then remembering herself she pulled away and thanked him profusely. Normally he would ask Aileen to fetch Alice to him and he would say his goodbyes to her and all the children, but not today, he couldn`t face it and he set off in the pony and trap with the breeze trying still to snatch his biretta.

Chapter 7

It was a great blessing to know there were still kind people in the world and Aileen found herself constantly sobbing whenever someone came to give them ---"something for your children" but it was noticed that they looked around furtively when they did this, would they never have peace? In the next weeks before their train journey again to Dublin, there was much to organise and so for that she was grateful to father O`Connell for his making all the arrangements for Alice. Padraic and Kelly their only remaining loyal officers had stayed to help with the clear up but clearly worried by their own involvements they had returned to their own families both in Waterford Bay. They had friends, thank God who made the arrangements for their passage to Holyhead. None of them had ever left Ireland and now they would be going to Wales first before travelling to Somerset in England. She wondered if the Irish would ever be able to have peace.

Her aged Mother and Father came to visit, something that they had not done for many a long time, but with a good friend to drive the trap they had come many miles. Her mother was dressed as if in mourning with her black skirt and black lace blouse. She greeted her daughter with a rather stiff hug and formal kiss on the cheek, with her husband it was an even more formal shake of the hand. Her father too with his moustache and great grey beard, he was unusually silent and tense. It was a tenseness borne of love and fear for their daughter and husband. All her grandchildren pecked at her cheek and spoke politely to their Grandmama, they were all rather subdued by her brusque attitude, and were allowed to kiss the cheek of their grandfather who was ever so slightly less scary. Surely, thought Aileen she knows that I have lost everything, as her mother tutted because they sat in the small kitchen that was part of their temporary abode. She wondered if her mother would be so generous to folks if the need arose. They drank tea from the best cups their host could provide and it seemed as if they were all present at a wake. Later as they were leaving her mother called to Aileen and held her in her arms. "God be with you, my dearest daughter--- send word as soon as you can" and then just as she was about to get into the pony and trap she turned in the direction of Alice "What you are doing for this one— it`s only right,---the institution is the place for her" and she resumed her stiff attitude. "Mama please--- don`t---we don`t want to talk of that---- not here—not now! ----and it`s not an institution" she was almost hissing the words to her mother, angry that the assembled children might hear. The grandchildren were all kissed and the twins whom she could never tell one from the other she clasped hands with, as they clearly were above hugs and kisses. Her mother just waved her gloved hand over her shoulder in the direction of Alice "Don`t be silly dear--- she can`t hear us!----goodbye everyone----goodbye!" and she was gone. Aileen felt sad that she felt nothing but relief that they had left and taking Alice by the shoulders, who was looking up with a puzzled face, they went back inside.

The farewell was both a sad affair but heart warming too, to think that they still had friends who cared for them. They had been given so much in terms of material possessions and often from folk who had the least to give. So there were many hugs and kisses and tears and promises to write and once again they found themselves on their way to Dublin. Liam sat back wearily listening to the wheels on the track and the whistles, the smell of the coal and steam hissing and soon his head lolled on Aileen`s shoulder. Alice was looking out of the window; she still did not know that she was not featuring in the move to England.

It should have been exciting to all be piling into the charabanc with all their luggage and being taken to Dun Laorghie and to take the mail boat to Holyhead. Instead Liam and Aileen were speaking sharply to the sobbing children and the twins were sniffing too. It wasn`t before that they had shown great affection for Alice, but their parents duplicity shocked them.

"Mama—Mama –why---why--- you didn`t tell us--- we didn`t understand--- why?" Bernadette was filled with rage, more that their mother had tricked them all into playing in the garden of her Aunt and Alice who had never played with the other girls next door before, was duped into a game of hide and seek, "She thought we were all hiding Mama--- that`s not kind---poor Alice" The others who had never before been able to criticise their parents--- or at least not in front of them---joined in. "That`s enough!" boomed Liam, eager to maintain discipline "---Enough--- it is a decision that was not taken lightly--- and t`is not something we need to explain to you---it is done and when things are settled ---we will fetch her back--- so no more--- it is upsetting your mother" and Aileen looked away, swallowing hard and praying that it was in fact the right thing.

The grey sea swelled on that autumn evening with the gulls crying and the smoke from the stacks of the steamer belching. They were all aboard courtesy of The Dublin Steam Packet Company, they and the many other passengers on the mail boat to Holyhead. Mr and Mrs Delaney were there at the pier waving and waving until they were dots and the vessel was well into the Irish Sea. Liam held his wife`s hand as the wind whipped her hair and she fought to keep her scarf around her shoulders. The boys ran off to investigate the vessel and the others all found a seat to ride out the hours ahead as the sea became rougher. Liam tried to make idle talk to while away the time and to also help him to concentrate on anything apart from the grey swell. " It will take time to get used to calling that place Dun Laoghaire, it has been Kingstown for so long --- but many names are changing"

"Mm-m –yes I know" she replied. " The service to Liverpool stopped last year---- and I am not sure if it will re-start—it was a great financial loss when the Leinster was torpedoed—""Always financial loss---what about those who lost their lives and there was the other ship that they owned---- that one sunk too!"

The RMS Leinster had been sunk by the Germans in the last war and approximately five hundred lives had been lost. Liam allowed some time to elapse before trying to make conversation again; he could sense Aileen was not in the mood to continue with small talk or current affairs. The twins always a bundle of energy rounded the corner and wobbled towards them looking very green and hastily Liam dragged them both to the rails and ducked their heads underneath, holding the scruffs of their necks as the wind whipped the white horses; the two copiously fed the fish. When they returned to their mother looking very grey, she searched in her bag for her smelling salts and her hand found a small packet wrapped delicately in tissue. She handed Liam her salts and he led the boys to somewhere where they could lie down. The wind wanted to snatch away the tissue and the label inside, but she hung on anxious to see who had slipped this package into her carpet bag. The sea spray was making the ink run, but she read "A little something to help you in your new life God speed. Love Mother and Father" It was easy to unwrap as the wind helped her, she laughed with a mocking tone "--- Oh and we won`t be starting our new life until we have used these I suppose---- Dear God Mother---!" and she regarded the little silver cake forks with their bone handles each blade had the double F monogram. "---Let us eat cake!" she thought. The sun coming from behind grey clouds suddenly shone on something between the layers of tissue, it was her grandma`s pearls. "Oh Mother—Mother--- I miss you already!" and as they headed out into the Irish sea, she felt that it might be a case of better the devil you know.

Chapter 8

Sister Imelda had seen many changes in her life and she had always loved her teaching, but nothing gave her more pleasure than the last ten years working with the deaf. The young girls in her charge had come from all over Ireland, some from England and there was one young girl who had come from America, her parents having sent her back to their native land. It always amazed her as to how resilient these girls were and how each adjusted to their level of disability, although it was never easy and hard for those who had remembered hearing. There were always the misconceptions, those ignorant people who for whatever reason, just didn`t understand and thought that raising their voices and shouting at a deaf person would solve all their communication problems. It was also the same with some of the parents, failing to acknowledge the difference between "hard of hearing" and "profound or total hearing loss". Most of her girls had a profound loss of hearing. Some had been born with their disability, perhaps it had been a premature birth and starved of oxygen, the damage had taken place, for others it was a result of illness, the brain fevers and the childhood ailments such as measles and mumps or it was a hereditary ailment with parents who were themselves deaf. In many ways, Sister Imelda felt it was better if the girl had been born with such a disability, then they did not know what they had lost. In Alice`s case it was found that she had almost a hundred per cent loss, sometimes she would jump if a door slammed, but it could not be determined if she felt, rather than heard it. In the test with her seated in front of a screen, a pair of cymbals were clanged together behind her and out of sight and Alice never flinched.

That day when she walked in to her office with her aunt and cousin, Sister Imelda had looked upon a frightened girl with the biggest blue eyes that she had ever seen. She had blonde wavy hair curling onto her shoulders and her fear and anxiety made her look very vulnerable. It appeared that her aunt had been made her ward and that her parents were in England, a few investigations led Sister Imelda to understand the nature of that. Poor child, she looked every inch like a frightened deer. It was agreed that she should be a boarder, even though she could have travelled to her aunt`s house each day, it was obvious that her aunt had little understanding, ability or more to the point, the time money, or inclination to take on a deaf child. She would however have some weekends with her and the school holidays. It was also understood her mother would visit when she could, but no dates had been made concerning this. So began her days and nights at the school. That night as she made her rounds the Sister peered into the dormitory of eight girls where Alice was sleeping, she turned to walk out and heard sobbing. It was Alice. She walked to her bed and sat beside her hoping not to startle her. When Alice turned and looked surprised to see her there, she took the child`s hands and squeezed them gently and moving to pat her brow she smiled, a smile that seemed to Alice to be that of an angel.

The next morning Alice was asked to go to the office of Sister Imelda. She was very nervous and timidly knocked at the door that was already open, so she could see the kindly woman at her desk. The door was always open; it was considered a stupid act to close it, for how could the girls know what the response would be. The deaf always have a problem with closed doors. She smiled and beckoned to Alice to come and sit down in front of her desk. The chair had a comfy cushion and a vase of pink roses was on her desk filling the room with an inviting scent. Gazing around she noticed the cross with the Blessed Lord Jesus and the statue of Mary, the Holy Mother. She always liked looking directly into the eyes of Mary and often addressed her prayers to the picture her mother had had in her bedroom. Alice doubted that the picture had survived the fire. To her embarrassment she realised that Sister Imelda had been trying to gain her attention, "I am s-sorry" she stumbled. The matter was waved away by kindly hands and Sister Imelda began to write and handed the paper to Alice.

My dear Alice, I know that you are away from your family. This must be very hard, but I want you to think of us all here as family. If you work hard, we will help you to adjust to your life. It will not be an easy life for you, I am afraid that deafness is often called the Unseen Disability—you have your sight and both arms and legs, you can walk and run, and to a degree, you can talk---- but that`s a problem--- it sounds different--- and you know how frustrating it is not to be understood and sometimes you will find there is a look of distaste that will cross a person`s face when they realise that you are deaf; as if it is catching. People talk about being stone deaf—I see it like this-- it is a stony silent path that you have You will have to walk---   be strong, you will have to have an outer strength and an inner peace. God`s love will give you that. I have been told that you love animals and nature and that you attend to your prayers and studies, I am pleased Alice .Continue to see that the world is full of God`s beauty and that although we don`t always understand his ways, He is there loving us always. Even the Holy Father in Rome, does not know all the answers to our questions. We say "Why did God make me deaf, why did someone we love suffer and die?"--- We only have to have faith and know that all will be answered someday. Did not God send his beloved Son Jesus to teach us that. Now, as for your voice, you will see here that we don`t use our voices, we just mouth the words so that the word shapes are clear and we lip read and use the sign language to enhance our language—do you understand all this?

She passed the paper to Alice and was pleased to see that she could read well and she nodded that she understood, although Alice was horrified to see the comments about the Holy Father in Rome and wondered if this was blasphemy, but in this room with this woman smiling at her, it seemed unlikely. She returned to her classes and soon started learning that she must not use her voice, it was hard to stop doing that and learning sign language was not so difficult as she had thought it would be. She learnt the alphabet on her hands and the signs seemed to relate well to the letter they portrayed, she also learnt that whole phrases could have just a few signs and some were to her very beautiful and often she felt that the signs conveyed the sense better than words. Some signs had historical significance, for example she was puzzled as to why tapping on her elbow with the palm of her hand signified the word biscuit. This was a reference to the sailors in Nelson`s day who had to tap the weevils out of their ship`s biscuit. The sign for sugar was a light tapping movement on her cheek. The workers from days gone by in the sugar factories often got a skin rash from the sugar and would have itchy faces. The sign for a woman, was to stroke her index finger from her hair line down to her jaw, indicating a ribbon from a bonnet and grabbing your chin and pulling down to indicate a beard, was the sign for a man. The sign for a dog was to pat the top of your leg in a sort of "here boy!" fashion, but patting further up on the hip could mean you needed the toilet! It was in all a lot to learn and adjust to.

The girl from America, Cynthia, had had some sort of brain fever and had become deaf two years before Alice and she was still very angry and often had rages and then sometimes she would fall onto the floor and shake. This was not only distressing for her, but frightened the other girls. Alice was popular and made friends easily, they practised their signs together and made cat`s cradles with their fingers and yarn, to keep their fingers supple for the signing. The thing that Alice missed most after her family was being able to hear stories read aloud, but she still had her love of reading and the school had a good library. As autumn passed and the days grew colder, she would take to sitting in the library by the fire instead of under the fruit trees in the garden. Sometimes Cynthia would join her, because even in their deafness they could still appreciate stillness and quiet.

One weekend Aunt Maggie was unable to have Alice at home and secretly Alice was glad because it was always awkward now, because her voice was altered considerably; it not having been used, no-one could understand her and they didn`t seem to want to try and learn to sign. Alice got frustrated and so did they because they didn`t speak slowly and enunciate their words, they forgot that she couldn`t be called for meals, that she couldn`t hear through a closed door and they got annoyed that they had to walk up to her if her back was turned to get her attention and if she was at the bottom of the garden, it was a long walk. Alice was getting used to being with deaf girls and becoming proficient in using sign language, so they could have whole conversations and she was communicating with girls of around her own age. She was one of the youngest at eight, but they all had lots to laugh and giggle at. That weekend they were told they were going to have a treat, a visit to the picture house. Alice had never been before. So she was very excited when they all got the tram and went to The Savoy on O`Connell street. It was very grand and the girls felt grand themselves in the sumptuous surroundings. Sister Imelda had told them that she wanted to take them to the Volta on Mary street, as that was indeed a very interesting picture house because James Joyce had opened it in 1909; but they weren`t showing the Chaplin films today. When the house went dark Alice became very excited and from the start was amused and enthralled by Charlie Chaplin. The funny little tramp with his twirling cane had such an expressive face and it was so easy to understand what was going on. It was a love affair that was to last for many years. Visual comedy being so important in her life she became a huge fan of Buster Keaton and the Keystone cops, right through to Morecambe and Wise, Tom and Jerry and her favourite, Mr. Bean.

They saw two films, the older film "A Dog`s life" and the newer film "The Idle class" and they laughed with tears streaming down their faces. "Did you enjoy that now?" asked Sister Agnes as she and Sister Imelda herded the girls out of the theatre. The rosy cheeks and smiling faces said it all.

About the Dominican Convent in Dublin, Eire, I was happy there. The nuns were nice and friendly and also the domestic people. The Chaplain was nice too, Father Flynn. I was there a few weeks and I got pains in my ears. I was put in the sick room, they had a special room with a nurse to look after us when we were sick. After I got better I was back at school. They had a large room where the juniors and the seniors were taught. We had a nice teacher to teach us.

Alice had woken a few weeks later with raging earache and had told Sister Agnes after she had woken from a bad night`s sleep. There was a yellow liquid coming from her ears as well so she was immediately hurried off to the sanatorium. The pain was very intense and the doctor who came commended her on her bravery. She would have to stay in bed for several days and lie with her infected ear on a pad of gauze whilst the abscess continued to drain. She felt very miserable, but gradually the pain subsided and the abscess healed but the doctor said that she would always be susceptible to further infections. Cynthia was the first to come and see Alice, furiously signing and asking when she would be back in the dormitory. The red headed, curly haired girl was fast becoming a best friend.

The other girls were pleased to see Alice back and one afternoon, another weekend at the school, Alice was told she had a visitor, thinking it was her mother she ran into the lounge and was sad that she wasn`t there, but then from another door came Jimmy! Alice flew into his arms and hugged him hard. He looked her up and down holding her at arm`s length he indicated her hair, which she had had cut when Aunt Maggie had taken her to her own hairdresser and it had been agreed that she could have the new short bob, that most women seemed to have adopted. It suited her and with her smart white dress and new shoes, she looked quite grown up and older than her eight years. She just beamed at him, but when he tried to understand her speech, he was shocked at how little he was understanding. She took his hands and tried to teach him the sign language, he tried but found his big fingers didn`t go the way she wanted them too. He promised he would try and she lent him a book to help him. He was pleased however to see that her lip reading was very good and he had already learnt to talk very slowly and clearly. She yelled with delight when he told her that Erin had had a baby girl. "Shona," he said, "We have called her Shona, Erin is well and the baby is a good size. I have seen the rest of the family and Grandma and Grandpa, and I have a letter for you from mama and Dada--- they went to London because our big brother Niall has been ordained ---and he is a proper Priest now all right! Can you imagine Mama`s joy--- and I should think that Father O`Connell will just burst with happiness. Well here—here is the letter." Although she was pleased to see Jimmy and to hear about her new niece and pleased for the brother whom she had hardly known, she was sad that her mother had only sent a letter. She would read it later. Jimmy wondered what his mother would make of the decline in Alice`s voice. She had convinced herself and others that this school would make her voice right. He had a feeling that her mother wanted to be able to present a child who sounded "normal". This then was going to be a huge disappointment. Jimmy promised that he would visit again soon and if Erin was up to it, they would come with the baby and Christmas would be here soon and maybe, just maybe she would be going to England for the holidays. Having said this, Alice jumped up and down and he hoped that this was so.

Alice read the letter that was not as long as she had hoped, it asked after her and hoped her ear pains were gone and that she was pleased to hear that she was doing well and that she would hopefully come at Christmas to take her to England. She wrote about her joy of going to London to see the ordination of Niall. Her mother gushed about the ceremony and pageantry, writing about the colourful robes of the cardinals and the Bishop. "I am so happy" she wrote. Alice was also happy that now her mother had something to be happy and proud about and it seemed they were well settled in England. "Good" she thought "I am glad"

Soon the preparations for Christmas were under way and the girls were allowed to go into the large kitchen to each have a stir of the Christmas pudding and to make a wish. Mrs. Miggins the large cook, like something from a Dickensian novel, so Alice thought, told them she would be adding the coins later. The kitchen had a wonderful smell and reminded her of her mother`s puddings that would steam for hours with their muslin covers. The girls were able to help with mince pies and in the afternoon they all donned hats and scarves and walked to the local park to gather fir cones and greenery to decorate the two large fireplaces. They also went to O`Connell street to buy presents for their families. That trip to Clery`s was very special, Alice loved that store with its grand classical columns and the clock above the doorways. It was looking splendid after it had been refurbished after the rebuild from the Easter uprising, the Sister`s were at pains to point this out. Alice was looking forward to Christmas with her family in England, so she bought a beautiful angel with real goose feather wings and hoped there would still be a tree like in the old days.

Then on the last day of the term Alice could hardly contain her excitement, the nativity play had been done, the masses, the parties, the giving and receiving of presents from staff and friends--- Alice was given a leather notebook and a fountain pen and a copy of Alice in Wonderland--- which Sister Imelda had written in the front ----- *Keep looking and wondering dearest Alice*   Dear Sister Imelda, how she loved her.

Then in came all the parents to join in the service around the tree and Alice ran to her mother. She looked very glamorous in a coat with a fox fur trim and her hair was so different, she had had it cut too. Alice knew about hairstyles from looking at the advertisements in the papers and magazines and this was definitely a bob cut with the new marcel wave. She was also wearing a black cloche hat with a black feather at a jaunty angle, Alice noticed the other girls looking. Her mother`s cheeks had filled out and Alice noted that the gaunt hollow look of her eyes had gone, but she still had that tight lipped look of anger. Alice wondered why she looked angry when this was a happy time. After the service, other parents saw Mrs. Regan and Sister Imelda enter her office together and the door was closed firmly, but it was commented upon that voices were raised.

When my mother came one day to take me over to England for the Christmas holiday, she came in looking lovely in her coat and hat. I was pleased to see she had not abandoned me. She was talking to Sister Imelda and Sister Imelda was explaining that I and the other girls do not speak with our lips, but use our hands to talk with. I could see Mama was displeased and angry. She was disappointed I wasn`t taught to talk. When we got back home to England, she told me I wasn`t going back. I was disappointed as I was happy there and had lots of friends, but I was happy to be back with my family too.

I never saw the dear nuns or the school after I left Dublin. I read in The Universe (Catholic publication) that it is no longer there.

Chapter 9

After the traumas of their exodus from Ireland Liam and Aileen had been surprised that the gentle countryside not so dissimilar from scenes that they had left behind, had calmed them, Midsomer Norton in north east Somerset; had given them a soft haven. Liam`s brother Michael was a keen dairy farmer, but getting on in years he had been glad of help with his herd. At first the family had all squashed into his house, but as they had known this was impractical and Liam was eager to see if there was anything in the village that they could buy or rent. He was still waiting to see what money would come to him from any pay out from the RIC, but that had still to be settled. In the meantime a house had become available on the north east side of the village. A pretty area with soft green fields and pleasant views, even the view of the coal spoil or the Batch as it was known locally, was not so displeasing. The twins pretended that it was a volcano ready to erupt. They were thriving with enough trees to climb and places to fish for tiddlers and tadpoles. They and the girls were doing well at the school. Aileen liked that it wasn`t so far from fashionable Bath, and the ten miles or so could be reached by train and the little station in the village served them well. Only her brother in law and his family knew what had happened to them, to everyone else they were that nice family from Ireland. Although the troubles were escalating on the emerald isle, it seemed that in this quiet corner, life could continue peacefully. Aileen was happy to help her sister in law with sewing and mending and they kept chickens and ducks on their own land. She had decided that this was going to be the last place she moved anything into, she told Liam straight that they would not be moving again. "You can take me out that door there in my coffin--- but I am staying here--- I want us to put down roots here." She had pointed at the kitchen door with its two halves like a stable door. The twins ducked under the top door and came running in and had to be reminded to take their muddy shoes outside.

Liam was looking healthier too, getting stronger each day and he had not thought that he would take to dairy farming as easily as he had. He still woke in the night sweating, thinking of the fire and the faces of the two who had instigated the whole episode. Generally he enjoyed walking amongst the gentle creatures and although not his beloved Ireland, the landscape would suffice to give his lungs his fill of country air. Aileen was busying herself with a group from the local church. She was involved with flower arranging and was also now involved with the Parish council. She wrote regularly to Maggie and wrote occasionally to Alice. She had received a pleasant letter from Jimmy and thanking her for the blanket and matinee jacket she had crocheted for the new baby, but she was disappointed that he had not really answered her questions about Alice`s progress. He had stated that she was well and that her ear infection was healed and that she attended well to her lessons, but he hadn`t said anything about her speech and that was what she had wanted to know about.

When Aileen left to go and fetch Alice home for Christmas, she had left the house in a frenzied hive of activity. She would be gone for a few days to see her parents, to visit Jimmy and then on to fetch Alice. Alice would have a room with Bernadette and Mary and Bridie would be in the room across the landing, the boys had an attic room and there were two further rooms, one for Liam and Aileen and a smaller room that we forever be referred to as the guest room. Everyone was doing what they could to make the house look "Christmassy" paper chains had been hung and a large tree was in the sitting room and they had all had a hand in decorating it. A nearby farm had provided them with a very large turkey and a goose, Aileen had made her puddings and iced a large cake. All that was needed for a happy Christmas was to have Alice home with them. When she and her mother arrived home the entrance hall was full of the fragrance of pine cones and pine needles, the scent of mulled wine wafted from the kitchen. There was much hugging and kissing, and Alice felt her siblings did care and had missed her. On the sea crossing and subsequent train journey, Alice had watched her mother, so pleased to be with her and her mother in turn stroked her daughter`s head or squeezed her hands but they spoke little and Alice sensed her mother was disappointed in her, but was afraid to ask the reason. Her father was the last to snatch her up and twirl her round. His eyes were brimming with tears and he kissed the top of her head. He turned to his wife who looked tired and strained. The children were anxious to show Alice around the house and Aileen reminded them all that they had both had a long journey, but they ran off with Alice anyway. Alone in the sitting room with a glass of mulled wine in her hand, Liam had the opportunity to ask Aileen how he thought things were with Alice.

"No-one had really told me that she would not be using her voice---- have you heard her Liam, it is so difficult to understand her--- she uses her fingers to talk and I had no idea--- I am furious---- I thought by now---well--- I just hoped for a difference." She held her hand to her face and seemed so sad and angry and Liam was at a loss as to what to say, eventually he placed his fingers to his lips and replied. "Shush, my dear, shush--- the children are happy to be together again---let`s not worry unduly over this Christmas period and see what can be done before she returns to school."

"She`s not going back Liam, oh no, she`s not,--- I have already said that, and besides with the troubles an all, I want her here--- it may not be in this village, but in this land at least and you promised that we would get another opinion—you promised Liam." He agreed that he had, but insisted that they had their family Christmas and they would talk again on the subject after the festivities.

When Alice gave her mother the angel for the tree, Aileen held it in her hands and felt such a rush of emotions, such a fragile thing this small angel and it seemed to sum up everything. A chair was fetched so Alice could, whilst stretching up and held by her father, place it with due ceremony atop festive branches.

It was very mild that Christmas and much as they had all hoped for a white Christmas, it was not to be, but it was a warm homely Christmas with much laughter and family games and although communication with Alice had stalled again, they found she was still very intelligent and enjoyed playing cards and word games. When it came to charades, she was delighted that she had knowledge of the latest books and her miming and acting skills were very good and needed no interpretation. Her parents noted how keen she was to please and how quickly hurt and withdrawn she became when she struggled with speech and found herself rushing off to get paper and pencil. Liam was far more relaxed when they had guests at the house, the neighbours were invited in and they he felt had to accept his family as they were and that meant accepting Alice too. Aileen he noted was constantly on edge. Alice was pleased that she had received a parcel from Jimmy and his wife, as well as from other relatives in Ireland; but it was his letter and gift that she treasured. He had sent a studio photograph of himself and his family. He looked very proud and was looking more like papa. He told her that Red was doing very well with them and was even walking to heel--- sometimes! Alice missed that dog very much.

Mama had been given a small white puppy, a west highland terrier that she called Tinker and he sort of made up for the lack of the lolloping dog that Alice missed so much. Together with the dog, she and her siblings would walk the country lanes and it was an excellent time for exploring, to get to know the place that they all now considered to be home. January passed and no-one had said anything to Alice about returning to school and she was beginning to get anxious now, so she asked her mother with her voice, with her fingers, with her pen and paper. "Mama, when am I going back to school, it must have started again---- Sister Imelda will be cross---- I will fall behind."

The shaking head said it all, "No Alice, no, you won`t be going back, I—we want to find another school—here in England--- somewhere where you can use your voice" the tears were copious, it felt almost worse than being left behind. She hadn`t said goodbye to Sister Imelda, she hadn`t said goodbye to her friends and she didn`t have any addresses, she couldn`t even write to Cynthia. She was distraught.

The family were attending the local church and Father Robert, who knew Father Niall in London, had become closely involved with the family. He was instrumental in helping them to settle in. They had received some items of furniture from people in the parish, some had been shipped to them from Aileen's parents. Father Robert had taken an interest in Alice and had found information about a highly acclaimed school for the deaf in Yorkshire. So plans were made for Alice to attend, but not before Liam had fulfilled his promise and he gained information about a specialist in ear, nose and throat ailments and had also arranged for Alice to go to London for an operation. It seemed to Alice that she had only just arrived and she was travelling again, in other circumstances she would have been excited to go to London, but she was still very sad regarding her schooling and was now petrified at the thought of another hospital visit. She thought that if she had to go, she would try to be brave and maybe when she woke up, she'd be able to hear; but it wasn't to be. Thankfully the staff were kinder and more able to address all the questions that her parents were posing, although the response was not as they had hoped. It was explained that her initial surgery had been quite severe and although they would not or could not apportion blame, it is always a delicate procedure with some degree of risk; where had they heard that before! The nerves and structures of the ear, nose and throat it was explained; all being so closely linked are susceptible to irreparable damage and it was with regret that this along with probably some level of oxygen deprivation, had led to her deafness. It was a bitter blow and one that Alice felt the hardest. So she and her mother returned to North East Somerset with heavy hearts.

It took time to sort out the details for the school in Yorkshire and Alice had contracted a heavy cold so she stayed at home with the family, clinging to the thought that at least she was still at home. January turned to February and the days grew colder and at the end of March there was a terrible blizzard that lasted for several days. It was a struggle to bring the cattle in from the fields, it was a struggle to get about and the road in and out of Midsomer Norton was impassable. The school was closed and it was a wonderful time for the children with snowball fights and sledging and Alice stood in the garden with the flakes settling on her fair lashes and thought how beautiful the white landscape was. She secretly hoped it stayed like that forever and then she wouldn't have to go anywhere else. They could still trudge to the church, where many of the local men had dug a path to the door and although they were still wrapped in coats and scarves, the lit candles and the scent of incense made Alice feel warm and contented, she gazed anew at the eyes of the Blessed Lady. Father Bob as he had told the children to call him, made a point of talking with Alice after the mass; he had seen her tasting the snow and allowing it to settle on her mittens. He seemed to have the knack of talking slowly and clearly and she found she could lip read him. "Each flake is different, Alice, there are no two ever the same—never, ever. Like us, so many of us and all different and beautiful to Him. God made us different to be special and never forget it. You understand this?" She nodded. Yes, yes she knew. She clung to this as she separated again from her family and found herself in yet another new environment.

Chapter 10

Life went on, my mother was looking out for a school that taught deaf children to speak and Father Bob told her there was one, but it was up in Yorkshire. My Mother wanted me to go to that school. So one day my mother and a friend of my mother came to take me to the school. It was in Boston Spa in Yorkshire. I thought the nuns would be friendly and nice like the ones in Dublin but they weren't. The nun took me into the kitchen and gave me something to eat and drink and then took me into the bedroom where all the girls were asleep in bed. My mother, Mrs. Munden and I, had travelled all day and it was night time when we got to the school.

I was very surprised to see that The Sisters of Charity were wearing a strange hat, it was a white winged hat like a birds wings. It was a copy of the head gear some peasants wear in France. I was scared.

So Aileen left again with Alice trying hard not to cry and for the most part succeeding, but her chin was wobbling as she waved from the window to her mother. Mrs Munden, Father Bob's housekeeper comforted Aileen as they started back home again "What have I done, what have I done?" She was told that she was doing the very best for her daughter, but it didn't feel like that at that moment. The nun with her strange head gear indicated her bed and Alice lay once again in the dark feeling desolate.

The girls were kind and soon embraced Alice into their close knit circle. They did talk, with slow open mouths, enunciating carefully, using their voices as best they could. There were fewer girls with total hearing loss, but they all were forbidden to use sign language. They were encouraged to read aloud and a great deal of time was taken in the explanation of grammar and letter sounds and having to learn all the strange exceptions to word pronunciation, bough, bow, cough, trough, and all the countless other nuances of English language, having to remember when "i" says its' own name and when not; thinking that she had a pronunciation and then to find out that the "p" was silent. Attempts were also made to help them understand the rise and fall, intonation and volume of their voices, something that would be a life long struggle for Alice. There were many words that she would never fully master, but her love of literature intensified regardless.

The school was a large old imposing building and easy to get lost in, but the gardens and surrounding countryside were magnificent and soon had Alice in her favourite pastime of poking about in the hedgerows and writing, she loved writing stories and letters that were very observant and all written in a beautiful cursive script.

The nuns were not like Sister Imelda, they were not given to such open displays of affection but for the most part they were caring if rather brusque in their manner and saw to the task of imparting spiritual and educational knowledge. There were girls like Alice who were homesick and some who had difficulty with the long nights and the wet sheets in the morning were a source of embarrassment, especially as they had to take them themselves to the laundry and give an apology to the laundry staff. It seemed to Alice that it was always cold there too and she loved the coal fire in the library and the oil stoves in the classrooms. She recounted in later life that she constantly had chilblains. So she longed for the warmth of summer.

One summer we had a sports day. I was commended for my running and jumping which was strange because we didn`t have sports lessons. We used to go for walks about the countryside. We used to look odd with a Sister in her head gear accompanying us. After our lessons in the classrooms, we used to go to a big play room. On the wall was a big black board where we children could write or draw anything. I started to draw, copying the girls. I liked drawing. The months went on with lessons. I was good at my lessons and got some prizes.

In the autumn the girls were allowed to go blackberry picking, but Alice was always eager to pick as many as she could and to reach the ones that the other girls gave up as being too difficult to reach. On one day Alice returned covered in a mixture of blackberry juice and blood from her badly scratched legs and arms. Her clothes had also become casualties. She was not greeted openly and was not allowed out for a few days as a punishment for her torn clothes. It was a hard punishment to the girl who loved to be communing with nature.

It was in the autumn that I was first there, that the girls and I, turned our thoughts to going home for Christmas, we didn`t go home very often, but we loved Christmas. The girls used to draw on the board, Christmas cakes, puddings and Father Christmas and always pictures of trains going home. I thought the pictures were excellent and I tried to copy them. We were not taught drawing, soon I got on better at drawing and was brave enough to put my drawings on the board. The older girls told me I was getting better. It was not only that we did drawing, we did dancing and acting.

Alice was still dancing into her eighties; she counted the rhythm in her head and could sometimes feel the vibrations of the music in her feet.

At school I liked acting better. Later, when I had been there for several months, the woman who came to supervise us, a very nice and friendly one; told me that the Sisters wanted us to put a play on and that I was to produce it. I was horrified and told her I was not good enough. She told me that she watched me and thought I was excellent. Soon the girls and I started to work on the play. I have forgotten the name of the play, but I remember that the day we put it on I was proud because we got a round of applause. I was thankful it was over I don't remember if my mother was there.

Although the school lacked the warmth of Sister Imelda the Sisters were good teachers and Alice was soaking everything up like a sponge, this was a good thing for they were inclined to treat the slower pupils with what Alice considered to be, undue harshness. She had her friends and one special friend named Molly and they liked to talk together about all manner of things, but they risked punishment constantly because they would constantly finger spell and sign with their hands, they had found this to be useful in areas like the library where they needed to be quiet. It was also useful in the dim light, late at night in the dormitory. There were a few letters from home and parcels and occasionally Alice went to stay with her uncle and his wife by the coast, Alice couldn't swim but loved the sea. She spent many hours just staring at it, amazed by the power of the moon upon its tides. She loved the cool water pulling at her feet, the sand and pebbles and the alien worlds that were opened up for viewing in the rock pools when the tide went out. She could be lost for hours just gazing at everything the coastline had to offer. The salt air filled her with energy and her cheeks became rosy, she was less inclined to colds and ear infections when she was there. It became a thrill to be told she was going there and she didn't mind that she was spending less of her holiday with her parents and siblings.

As the years passed Alice was changing, becoming a stronger person with her own ideas and interests, she was popular and a very pretty girl; but she was like many of the girls still naive about many things. The inevitable changes to her body and the visit of the monthly curse had her feeling scared, embarrassed, thinking she was dying and after her friend Molly had explained a few things; she was angry that neither her mother nor her sisters had told her anything. As for where babies came from Molly's explanation was abhorrent to her and she decided that Molly had probably got that all wrong.

There was much excitement one spring when they were told that the whole school would be going on a pilgrimage to Lourdes in France. The story of St. Bernadette of Lourdes was one most of the girls knew anyway, but it was revisited and the girls held hopes for their own healing. It was a trip that was organised with military precision and one that the school had been making for many years. So the excited girls and the Sisters arrived in Lourdes. Here the Sisters in their elaborate headgear did not look out of place, as the girls witnessed many forms of religious garments; but it was the children who were crippled or paralysed that scared them slightly. The erratic movements of some and the wild staring eyes of others left them trying not to stare. They were all hoping and praying with more fervour than they had ever done before, rosaries in hand, hoping that they would become blessed and cured. Each girl said afterwards that although they had not become cured or had not seen any apparition of the Blessed Virgin that they had felt a very special peace and a stillness that stayed with them long after they returned to Yorkshire. The intensity of the visit to Lourdes over, they were able to have a few days in the French countryside and to enjoy the good food and scenery. Alice made several other trips to Lourdes as an adult and still recounted the feeling of inner peace.

In her last year at the school Alice worked exceptionally hard in all subjects, desperate to gain good marks and please her parents as well as herself. She had no idea what she would do after leaving school, she would have liked to be a writer, but she didn`t know how she would go about that. She had for the most part been cocooned within the school. Her hard work and attention to her studies paid off, because she was awarded top marks for her year group. She was presented with a copy of "Bible and Church History stories" and inscribed in the front it said *" Prize for highest term marks July 1928".* It was something that she showed to her parents and glowed with pride.

About Boston Spa Yorkshire, I stayed there for about four or five years. I got on fairly well with my lessons. I do not think the Sisters of Charity are teaching at Boston Spa now. I heard the school has changed and the children are taught by civil teachers.

Chapter 11

When Alice left the school in Yorkshire, Aileen had to accept that there was a small degree of improvement in Alice`s voice, but it had been made clear to her, that this was as good as it would ever be and that it would always be difficult for those who did not know her, to engage in easy conversation. Her family could always indicate when she needed to lower the volume or the intonation was all wrong. Alice was still frustrated that none of them would learn sign language. Despite this, it was good to be at home again and to be able to go walking with her mother`s dog and the two Labradors that had joined the family. The relationship between Alice and dogs was very special; the labs especially seemed to have certain sensitivity with her. She got into her mothers` bad books on several occasions for allowing the dogs in the house. Dogs belonged outside in the yard, and had their kennels for shelter. This was the Irish way or at least in this family.

For a few years Alice stayed at home with her mother, helping in the home and sometimes helping on the dairy farm. She watched and learnt as her mother taught her to bake and to sew. She was still an avid reader and now that she had more time she started to keep a diary. Something she continued to do daily and was still doing up to her ninety third birthday. Each morning and each evening she would kneel by her bed in prayer and say her rosary and attended the church services with her family, it was what was expected but for Alice it was more than just duty. There was one particular thing that troubled her however, she knew and her sisters knew that Alice had to be given some sort of employment, for her own sake and future and also to help with the family`s finances; but she couldn`t readily see what she could do and these were hard times. The depression had hit and men were queueing for jobs. They had read in the papers of the dock workers hammering on the doors of the Overseers and how they in turn had locked and bolted the doors, afraid for their lives. It was hard for the farmers in the area as the price of milk and meat had plummeted and there was little money to spend on such items anyway. There was nothing in the way of shop work to be offered in the village.

I settled down at home and the years passed until my father was seventy years old. My sisters asked my mother what she was going to do about my training for a job. My sisters said to me that Father is getting old and he isn`t going to be able to support you now that he is older. It was the same for them but they were teaching. Mama said she was definitely against me working in a factory, she said "There will be no factory job for you" I wondered why she said this because one of my deaf friends worked in a factory and I had met some of the people she worked with and they were all nice people and treated her very well. I told her so, but she still said No. I still liked to brush mama`s hair and was good at styling my sisters` hair *too, so my sisters said to my mother; why can`t she work as a hairdresser. Mama took me round to see the hairdressers but they were sorry they couldn`t have me, there was no work for all of them. Then she heard about a shop in Bath that train hairdressers so she took me there and I got a job. It was called the Bath School of Hairdressing and I stayed there for several months.*

It didn`t take long to travel on the train each day to Bath and Alice loved her new profession. She was a keen learner and discovered her flair for all the new styles that had come into fashion, the bobs and curls, the ever popular marcel wave. It was difficult sometimes with communication, but the woman who ran the school was patient and kind and thought that Alice lip read very well. That was something that had been a bonus of her education in Yorkshire.

"Pay attention to the customer`s reflection in the mirror, keep asking them if the style is right, the length etc--- it is important Alice that you don`t forget to talk to them and keep a pad of paper handy for them to write down their instructions to you if they need to do that---- because you are deaf, they need to feel confident with you---- but I am pleased with you Alice, tell your Mother that you are doing very well." Alice was bursting with happiness because she was holding her own, coping in the hearing world. In her lunch breaks she would walk along Walcott Street or stroll down by the river and sometimes she met a friend for coffee in the little cafe by the Abbey. She had a little wage, not much but she could give some to her parents and had some for a few luxuries and it made her feel that she had entered the outside world. But once she had qualified, the school could not keep her on and they sadly explained that it was always going to be just for the duration of her training, but she had qualified and that still meant the world to Alice.

When I left, I was looking for a job. I found one at Frome, it was a family hairdressing salon; I was there a few months, but I left I did not like it, they did not understand me. I found another hairdressers and worked there but I found the toilet was dirty and the owner was not truthful, so I left---- my mother was cross that I did not settle, but I was not understood. A few weeks later I was happy to find work in Bath again and I worked hard there but some months later they told me they were moving to Australia, so I was out of work again. I was glad because I didn`t mind not working there as I never told Mama, the man was crafty trying to make love to me when his wife wasn`t about.

She did not know his name, they must have been introduced but as often happened, she did not get it and was too shy to ask for it to be repeated. It was not important she made it her business not to have any need to address him. The first day that she had arrived at the salon she had been excited at being back in Bath and the pleasantries that the city afforded, but he had sullied her exhilaration. The owner of the shop had welcomed her with much flamboyant gesturing, an ample bosomed woman with a penchant for too much make up and an overpowering use of perfume. She talked too fast and her ever moving red lips were difficult to read. She was Alice thought, a nervous woman who used her hands to emphasise what she was saying, but they were mostly empty signs which confused Alice. She had that annoying habit that some people have of placing her hand in the small of Alice`s back and pushing her forward into the space in front of her. "Well, this is the salon" she said, that much did not need interpreting. She lit a cigarette and drew heavily on it as she flapped her arms around indicating the lotions and potions, all of which Alice was familiar with and thought this woman was slightly reckless with her cigarette so near to the pungent concoctions. She showed Alice where to find the towels and where to wash the brushes and combs etc., and where to take the towels for the laundry.

All of these items were housed in a small cupboard to the back of the salon and reached through a curtain and to the left of a toilet and a flight of stairs leading to the owner's private flat. The flamboyant woman then asked Alice to show her, her hands. She turned them over with a satisfactory nodding of her head, "Good, good, it is important to always be clean". She swept around fussing and handed Alice a list of clients arriving that day and what they would be requiring. Alice was suddenly aware that a man had entered the salon he must have come down the stairs and through from the small room at the back where the store cupboard was. He was staring at her and she felt a chill run down her spine. She did not know this man, she had never met him before; but he had a look,--- she was thinking back, why did it unnerve her--- and realised it was the look not dissimilar to the looks she had been given all those years ago, first in her garden as a small child and then later by the same men at the barracks. If the devil existed she felt that she had met him before and now here he was again. He lounged against the door jamb with a cigarette in his hand, he had dark oily hair that flopped in front of his eyes and was wearing a singlet and dark trousers. Dark hair grew under his arm pits and sprouted around the top of his singlet. Alice felt that this was a most improper state of dress or in fact, undress, to be around ladies in a hair salon and maybe this woman should be looking at how clean he was! His wife, as that was what the flamboyant lady was, must have said something like "This is Alice,--the one I told you about,-- but for heavens` sake, go and put something decent on!!" and annoyed, ushered him out. He turned slowly to walk away and do what she had commanded but his eyes continued to stare in a menacing way and with his wife`s back to him, he winked and blew Alice a kiss. For most of her working days, he was not around. She was never sure what it was he did exactly; he would often be gone before Alice arrived and come back just as the salon was being shut up. If he walked in as she was tidying up, his stare made her clumsy and he knew it, he seemed to delight in seeing her flustered and receiving a telling off from his wife. He was still winking and leering at her over his wife's shoulder.

Alice tried to forget him and in her lunch break would walk again to Poultney Bridge and watch the rush of water over the weir, or walk on along the tow path to feed the ducks. It was one lunch time when she strolled in the warm sun, when her heart stood still, it was him. He was sitting on the grass under a tree and had his arm around a rather pretty young girl. They were giggling and laughing and she kept batting his hand away from her chest and was making half hearted attempts to stop him kissing her neck. It was very lewd behaviour for a public place and besides what on earth would happen if his wife found out, thought Alice. That was their problem and right then and there she wanted to be as far away from him as possible and hoped he did not see her. Luckily he was too occupied to notice her. When she re-entered the salon her employer was puzzled and tapping her watch mouthed "You're early or keen--- you're back early!" but Alice didn't mind, her heart was still thumping as she washed her client's hair. He didn't feature much for the next few weeks, his wife was busy telling her ladies that he was in London "sorting things out" she meant to tell Alice soon about their emigration. "Poor girl!" she thought "She'll be heartbroken and where is she going to get another job—it isn't easy for her being deaf and dumb" She said as much to her clients, even with Alice present, because she could.

On Wednesdays the shop was closed for business, but the towels had to be washed which took almost the whole day with the boiling and rinsing and then wringing them through the mangle and then when that was done there were the brushes and combs to be washed and the salon floor to be mopped. It fell upon Alice to do all this and the ruby lipped woman would have business in town. One afternoon she had just hung out the towels in the garden and was coming back into the back store room, when he appeared standing in the doorway with the curtain behind him. He smiled showing crooked teeth and came towards her saying something that she imagined was crude. Alice tried to push past him, but he blocked her exit into the salon, with his right arm, she tried to duck underneath, but he pushed her back against the wall near to the door to the garden. He gripped her shoulders and shoving her hard with her back thumping the wall, he tried to kiss her. Her fists came up and hammered against his chest, but he pinned them to her sides in a crushing embrace. His face was close to hers and his mouth with its foul breath was skimming hers trying to gain a purchase on her lips, but she shook her head violently from side to side and was screaming. His eyes were fixed on her and he grinned. It was when he allowed one hand to slip down to her skirt and his attempts to lift up the material, that her own arm became free and she brought it up and slapped him hard. He raised his hand to slap her even harder, but he suddenly dropped it and walked past her into the garden. His wife had come back and he had heard the bell on the door. Alice was now aware of his wife`s movements in the shop and did not want to be seen in this dishevelled manner, neither did she want to say anything. What if he said she led him on?. She had problems enough with communication with this woman and was too scared to broach the subject, so she quickly went to the toilet and re-arranged her hair and clothes. She never saw him for the rest of that afternoon, he must have climbed over the low wall in the back and out into the alley behind and his wife didn`t enquire where he was.

"Oh there you are Alice--- I wondered where you were" she beckoned to Alice to come and sit beside her and shaking, Alice did so. "Oh dear Alice, don`t look so nervous--- no---um----you`re not being told off---n—no. It`s just that we are going to Australia soon and um---well there won`t be any salon here. So well---I am sorry--- because you work hard." Everything that had just passed welled up inside Alice and she burst into tears. "Oh shush now—oh Alice--- I am so sorry, so sorry---I`ll make sure you have good references----don`t cry!" but Alice had made up her mind and snatching up some paper she wrote. "Thank you for employing me, but I am not feeling well so I think it is best if I leave today."

"Oh no Alice –you misunderstand—you don`t have to leave today" her employer was protesting, sad that she had made the girl distraught, she didn`t think they had been that close.

The door slammed and the bell jangled violently as she walked out and never went back. Alice didn`t hear it.

Chapter 12

Those eyes thought Alice, those eyes. She had seen the evil in his eyes and it was the stare that she had seen before, so many evil people. It made her daily devotionals even more poignant.

Her mother and her sisters were not withholding their anger and frustration and her mother said it wasn't Alice's fault that the owners were emigrating, but what was to happen now? The sisters alternated between caring and despairing. It made Alice feel once more that she was a burden. It turns out however, that even in a depression women still want to look their best and some money seemed to be made available from meagre housekeeping to afford a simple hair do. Alice had started providing a service in people's homes, a pudding basin cut for little Johnny, a shampoo and set for the lady of the house and was happy to trim a beard or moustache for the man of the house, but only if the wife was present. She was still wary around men, but for onlookers she was just Alice, a gentle quiet soul, a trifle shy, difficult to communicate with and wasn't it all sad for her and her family. For Alice it meant she was working again and could contribute a little to the housekeeping. Her mother had a local woman come in to help with laundry. Aileen told her daughters that like many families "She is struggling". The euphemism that summed up the plight of many families at the time and with the local coal mine in decline the hardship was evident. Aileen had taken to helping distribute the food packages from the Church harvest Festival and Alice often went with her. The row of miner's cottages fascinated them both and wondered at how they managed to squeeze all the family into such a small space and for the most part the homes were clean and tidy, but it seemed ironic that the families of miners struggled to keep their own homes warm and that food was scarce. Aileen felt it was her duty to be charitable but when she was told that some of the families had pleurisy, she told Alice firmly that there would be no more visits. A shame as Alice enjoyed cuddling the babies, she found that babies and small children would coo and smile and didn't realise she couldn't hear them. A smile after all is a smile and they always responded. She told her mother that perhaps she could help with the children whilst the mothers were ill, but her mother looked horrified and strictly forbade such contact.

Aileen had standards to uphold and she employed them rigorously. She insisted that on every day, snow and ice, notwithstanding, the windows of each room would be opened to allow the room to be fully aired and to rid it of germs. The household would shiver, whilst bedding was pulled back on the beds and rugs beaten and definitely no dogs in the house! Once a week she instructed Alice in how to clean the silver, she had her own now and had *R* in a scroll on the fiddle back spoons. The coppers were cleaned and she taught Alice how to cook. She told her "Tis the way of the Irish, always cook more than you need, and keep a welcome for all folk" and somehow she did, but the welcome only extended to family and close friends. You never knew what germs people might have, but still she lit the candle in the window each night, a welcome home, the way of the Irish.

Some evenings the family gathered around the piano and Aileen would play and on a few occasions Liam would even condescend to sing, his greying whiskers masking his mouth and even in singing a silly song he remained a figure of stature. It no longer seemed cruel to sing or play music in front of Alice and she would place her hands on the frame of the old upright and watch the hammers strike, feeling the vibrations. If there was dancing she would join in and enjoyed the chance to be frivolous with the family.

The years passed by and Alice remained at home whilst her sisters married and her brother Sean married too and broke his mothers heart by moving away to America. The twins who as always were a single unit, but with more striking differences now, Jack had a ginger beard and moustache and Tom just sprouted a moustache. The day that they had both enlisted in the Royal Navy, they stood before their parents identical once more in their clean shaven state. Aileen appealed to her boys with her customary handkerchief in hand "I suppose there is no use in asking for a change of heart, you both have made your decision, I can`t say we are happy----"

"We are proud of you both, that we are," interrupted Liam, "We will always be proud and ask God to bless you both--- isn`t that so Mother?"

"Yes" she replied and hugged them both close. When Alice came to hug them too, she suddenly found herself weeping uncontrollably and felt a sense of foreboding. She could not look at her mother.

There were many changes taking place in people`s lives, there were more cars on the roads, some including Alice`s family had gas lamps installed and now a new thing had arrived in their family, a wireless receiver. A tuned radio frequency receiver to be exact and it seemed to Alice to be a thing that was revered. Obviously it had no attraction for her, she was told that it could produce music and that voices could be heard, but it was just a piece of furniture to be dusted and an annoyance to her as she would sometimes enter the room, eager to tell her parents something and her voice would be exceptionally loud and her intonation all over the place; she would be faced with fingers to lips and angry faces shushing her or flapping hands waving her away and indicating sit down and be quiet!! Her evenings changed as her father would sit and read the paper and her mother would be sewing or reading and the thing in the corner was listened to. The piano seemed to be used less and the family gathered around that thing in the corner. It was only cinema that interested Alice and even though she was missing the speech, she still loved to watch films and saved hard to enable her to go at least once a week. She cared less about George V giving a Christmas broadcast or the young Princess Elizabeth, and found herself being hauled to her feet whilst something called the National Anthem played. She brought the King to mind and taught herself to adopt a reverential face.

The scissors were still snipping away in the village, but Alice was restless wanting to earn more money and to have a proper job and then someone told her mother about a job at a hairdressers in Bristol in a place called Castle Street. So Alice travelled on the bus to Bristol and armed with written references she went for her interview. She was pleasantly surprised to find that the woman interviewing her spoke slowly and clearly and wrote things on a pad of paper when there were any specific details that needed emphasising and she was happy to have Alice on board as part of her team of hairdressers. Alice was happy, determined that whatever came she was sticking to this job and although it meant getting up early to enable her to get the bus for the long trip each way, she was working harder than ever, finding her colleagues helpful and caring towards her and her clients for the most part pleased with her and most made an effort to communicate. It was also a lively part of Bristol to be working in with its shops and lively atmosphere, many shops opening late into the evening some not closing until ten, and people happily strolling around enjoying an evening out. There were numerous coffee houses including one that Alice liked to go into on her breaks, the Star coffee house had a warm atmosphere in its Victorian grandeur a five storey imposing building with a small dentist next door. Sitting in there she again felt like an independent woman. In the busy evenings people strolled enjoying a drink in the pubs and the shops were exciting with Woolworths, Marks and Spencer, Boots and some small retailers with their smart awnings. The narrow street was closed to traffic due to the crowds that gathered and only the tram still ran. There were numerous barrow boys and at the end of the days` trading, it was possible to buy meat at reduced prices as obviously there were no freezers to keep the meat in. So this would be an occasional treat for her parents when she arrived home with a choice cut of meat. The area had a great magnetism and for those just coming out of hard times it was a wonderful evening adventure.

The shops also gave Alice an insight into the world of fashion, and although she was not earning a great salary she saved hard to be able to buy herself some items that would add to her wardrobe. She was very good at finding accessories and using them to change or enhance what she was wearing. She was certainly no plain Jane, but still she was very much a loner.

Not long after Alice got her new job, a letter arrived at home to say that Jack would be home on leave and was going to be bringing his fiancé to meet them all. Aileen went into overdrive and her thin lipped look was back again.

"Why has he not told us about this, we know nothing about this woman, he should have asked us before getting engaged,--- is she catholic? –we don`t know. Where are they staying—I am really angry---I want to see Jack, but I want my boy to myself----what—what are you giving me that look for? Can I not have an opinion now?"

Liam shrugged his shoulders and simply replied "Let the boy get here and don`t be interrogating the woman,--- give her time"

He knew that the tight lipped face and the sighing meant that the poor girl was in for a hard time, but it did pose many questions and he had the feeling of fireworks to come.

Chapter 13

One crisp autumn evening Alice worked later than usual and rounded the corner to see the back of her bus pulling away. Fortunately for her she knew that there would be another in an hour's time at nine o'clock. So she welcomed the opportunity to go for a coffee in the beautiful Star coffee shop. She found a vacant table on the ground floor and sat sipping her coffee and chose to eat a Danish pastry. She watched people come in and out, noticing the way people sit together, observing the way that those she suspected were in love with each other, leant across the table and stared adoringly at each other, perhaps a hand was held across the table; eyes shining and bright. She wondered about her chances of finding someone to maybe marry, she would very much like to have children, but wondered if that was possible with a hearing person. Would it be fair on them? What about children? She had been told that her condition was an accident and would not affect her children, but would any hearing person even be interested in her? She hadn't even had a boyfriend so she wondered why she was even thinking this way. She kept glancing at her watch because she knew that if she missed the next bus there would not be another that night. For her also, she had a very difficult time with time. When all is silent around you, it is difficult to gauge the passage of time. That might seem strange, but a hearing person has the advantage of overheard conversation, the radio, the chimes of a nearby clock, in a silent world, a deaf person needs markers in time and for Alice it had been known for her to miss appointments and the occasional bus!

It was whilst she was checking her watch, that on looking up she saw two figures enter and immediately she recognised her brother Jack. She stood up to go to him and saw that he was accompanied by a very glamorous woman, she realised she was staring. The woman was a little taller than her brother, with blonde hair that was Alice suspected the product of a good dye; never the less it suited her in its honey blonde hue. She had a soft perm in light waves that lightly touched her shoulders, all escaping from a red felt cloche hat. She wore brown leather gloves and a coat with a fur collar and fox head attached. Alice didn't care much for that, but noted that the woman was indeed very stylish. She had a pale complexion and very red lips. "Mama would not approve thought Alice, she looks like what mama calls a "loose woman". She also noticed that as they entered, the way her mouth moved was different from the way most people spoke. Alice knew about accents although of course she had no knowledge of their sound, and knew that it made it more difficult to lip read some people, but she just felt sure that this woman wasn't local. Jack spotted Alice and paused amazed to see her there, but was immediately ushering the woman towards her table. He held out his arms and hugged his sister and his female companion looked on curiously as he spoke without any voice emphasising his lips with each sound as he asked Alice what she was doing there and the formalities of how she was etc.

"Oh, sorry Bella,---this is my sister Alice---- um---you probably realise that she is deaf" Alice wondered when he suddenly became more interested in communicating in this way, he was always so rushed and found it annoying to have to speak slowly and clearly. She guessed he had grown up and was also trying to impress, but she was still very pleased to see her handsome brother. He removed his trilby hat and set it down on a spare chair at the table.

"Hi Alice!" she said and shot her gloved hand across the table, "I`m Bella, Jack`s fiancé." Alice didn`t manage to lip read her name and looked to her brother and said her customary "What?" which her mother kept reminding her not to say—"Pardon, Alice, Pardon." Jack told her again slowly forming the letters "B-E-L-L-A, her name is Bella, short for Isabelle" Bella took a small silver lighter from her clutch bag and offered Alice a cigarette, she declined because she did smoke occasionally but didn`t want Jack to know. Alice watched as he took the lighter lit two cigarettes and handed one of them to Bella. It was just like a scene from the cinema and she thought she was acting too much like a starlet. Bella smiled sweetly at Alice and leant forward and very slowly forming each letter sound she said "I am very pleased to meet you Alice, I hope we can be friends." It was the ice breaker. It touched Alice that she was making the effort. She turned to her brother and asked "Where is she from?" Jack frowned a little and corrected Alice "You mean, where does Bella come from? She comes from Boston America, we met a few months ago introduced by a friend of mine." "Oh" said Alice, warming to her but still a little wary. It turned out that she was working in theatre an actress near to where he was stationed and as Jack put it "Love at first sight Alice, love at first sight!" Alice was bemused but pleased for her brother. It bode well for Bella that she took the trouble to ask about her, fascinated by her hairdressing, remarking on the mother of pearl brooch that she had pinned to her cardigan. These details mattered.

Suddenly Alice panicked remembering her bus, she looked at her watch and said "Oh my bus--- I will miss it---- goodbye!" and headed for the door. Jack stood up and gently grabbed her by the arm. "It`s ok Alice--- don`t worry, we can take you back in Bella`s car" Bella started to look concerned. "I thought we`d see your folks tomorrow, thought that`s what we agreed?" Jack patted her arm and reassured her that a day earlier would be ok. Bella wasn`t sure that anytime was going to be a good time and Jack knew this too, but felt they`d better get it over with and maybe walking in with Alice would soften things.

Alice just felt that it was amazing that this woman had a car. She followed them both to where the car was parked, it was a car that made her draw drop. It was the sort of car she would imagine a film star to own. They drove home through the darkened evening, Alice holding her hair as it blew in the rush of air as the open topped car sped recklessly along the country lanes, braking hard as three chickens fluttered squawking across the road as they rounded a bend. "Slow down Bella, slow down!!" Jack yelled. "Oh Alice" she yelled back "Isn`t he a scaredy cat!" but Alice hadn`t heard and was just enjoying the adrenalin rush that came with being so reckless.

When they arrived at the home Alice went ahead and Jack put his finger to his lips and shaking his head to indicate don`t tell Mama and papa we are here. Her parents were in the lounge and realised something was up because Alice was grinning like a Cheshire cat. " What is it Alice?---- we were beginning to worry-- you are late!--- did you miss the bus?" Aileen had pointed at the clock and then saw movement in the hall and she beamed as she saw her son and went to him arms out stretched and then stiffened as she saw his companion. Straight and tall, lips thin she took in the woman who was wearing far too much lipstick for her liking.

"Mama this is Bella." And Jack was striding towards his mother and placing a hand in the small of Bella`s back he un-intentionally propelled her forward in front of his mother. "How d`you do. It`s a pleasure to meet you---- Jack has told me so much about you all. I just love this little village or what we have seen in the dark so far---" She realised she was rambling. "Isabelle, is it." Aileen asked like some Victorian matriarch. Alice could sense her mother`s disapproval and hoped her mother would not be so harsh. Liam had shot his wife a look and bade them all to come and sit and he engaged in conversation with his son asking about how long he would be with them, what he had been doing etc. Aileen sat watching this woman who suddenly seemed quite awkward fiddling with her bag. Coats removed and Alice was sent to put them on her bed for the time being, even her mother realised that this coat with the fox fur couldn`t just be hung in the cupboard of the hall. As Alice left the room her mother mimed making a pot of tea and Alice nodded. In the middle of a father, son conversation Aileen turned to Bella and bluntly asked. "Are you a Catholic?"

"Uh—n-no Ma'am I`m not, my family are church goers `tho. My mama and grandparents are all Baptists and I go along sometimes--- "

"She`s not a Catholic Jack--- did you know that? What are you thinking--- I hope she knows that she will have to convert?" Her eyes moved to Jack and did not look back at Bella. "Mama please, I hoped you would be more civil and give my fiancé a fairer, warmer welcome."

"Tell your mother Jack, tell her--- you may as well--- let`s get all the upset right now!" Bella was imploring with Jack, her hand to her mouth and holding back tears.

"Mama, papa we won`t be marrying in the church---"

"What!" screamed Aileen "Liam--- d`you here what our boy is saying?"

""Quiet Aileen--- let the boy finish" Liam`s hand was raised and he stood to stand by the fireplace, reaching for his pipe.

"Firstly, I just want to say that I am not a boy, I am a man, I am 28 years old and I have chosen Bella to be my wife. You have always said that everyone is welcome in this home, I did not think you would act this way----
"

"Show some respect!" boomed Liam.

"Papa. I will, but please respect us too--- mama I never imagined that this conversation would be easy, I have always respected the church and never wished to go against all that it stands for but I cannot marry in Church even if I had chosen too—"

"What do you mean?" Aileen`s voice little above a sob.

"I`ll tell you, I`ll tell you why no Catholic church would marry us---- I am divorced! I am three years older than Jack and I was divorced two years ago--- it was not what I had wanted ---but—" Bella was on her feet and with voice raised in anguish.

"Go, both of you go, I will not talk of this further, you realise that you have sold out your soul to the devil, that you will be damned, that your soul will rot in hell---- just go!" Aileen had found her voice again and was screaming with tears running down her face as Alice appeared in the doorway with the tray of tea things. She stood open mouthed and trying to understand why everyone looked so stunned.

"Tell us, tell us about your divorce" Liam asked of Bella.

"That`s none of your business, she doesn`t have to tell you her personal details!" screamed jack.

"Alice for heaven`s sake come in and put the tray down, stop gawping!" Aileen beckoned to Alice to place the tray on the small side table. Alice was distraught seeing the faces and the screwed anguish on each and not being told what was going on.

"No I`ll tell you, I`ll tell you--- but I doubt that it will make any difference to your opinion of me. Yes I was married and now I am divorced, my husband was a lovely man to start with and then he started to lock me in the house and if I hadn`t prepared his meals or done the things he asked to be done properly and there was no pleasing him----well then he beat me-----" she broke off to dab at her eyes.

"These things happen---- sometimes in a marriage--- you have to make allowances--- not that I have encountered this---but I know many who have--- it is a wife`s duty to stand by her man---"

"Mama please!! Bella is telling you intimate things and you reply with no feeling! I think the matter is closed--- we will be married in a registry office and after this---- we will do it as soon as possible!" Jack was incensed. Alice was sobbing, but she didn`t know why.

"You had better make arrangements to stay in lodgings, you can`t stay here. I must say I am disappointed Jack, deeply disappointed--- you have disgraced the family and if you continue with this lunacy--- you will not be welcome here." Liam continued to puff on his pipe and regained his old military stance.

Jack went to kiss his mother, but she waved him away, his father just stared into the grate. He took Bella`s hand and went to get their coats and realising that they were in Alice`s room, reminded him that his sister had no idea what was going on. He took her hand and led her outside to where the car was parked. He hugged her realising that there may not be many more opportunities to see her. He wanted to get Bella away as fast as possible and didn`t want to go into long explanations that would be tedious to explain to Alice and did not have the energy to enunciate each word. Bella realising his anguish whipped out a small note pad and with a pencil hastily wrote.

"Alice, sorry it is like this, I like you and am sorry we have made your family sad. I was married to a bad man who hurt me and I am divorced, you know I can`t marry in your Church. I would like you to be at our wedding a civil ceremony, will write with details--- please pray for us."

Alice reeled in shock, she was not sure what could be so bad that her parents had sent them away. This revelation left her breathless. She knew that her brother would now be a non Catholic in the eyes of the Church and that he wouldn`t really be married. She didn`t know what to think about it all. She loved her brother, she was feeling mixed emotions for this woman; on the one hand she had tried to be interested in Alice and appeared to care, but she was a divorced woman; which was scandalous. She was not sure about attending the wedding. It would be a sham. She hugged her brother and then felt a wave of sadness for this woman, Bella had been hurt, was it her fault that she had fallen in love with her brother? She held out her hand, but Bella pulled her in to her and clung to Alice sobbing on her shoulder. "I`m so sorry Alice, I`m so sorry!"

Alice watched them drive away, a shame she thought, there was someone who could have been a really good friend to have and her brother, her lovely brother damned for all eternity! She turned to walk back into the house, knowing that the air would feel heavy and the words unheard would reach her anyway.

Chapter 14

The leaves had long fallen, the russets and golds that normally held such an attraction, were hardly noticed this season. Walks with the dogs were mere necessities and Alice was suffocating under the invisible blanket of immeasurable anguish that seemed to be wrapped around the inhabitants of her home. Her mother wore it most, more stooped in appearance these days; but still with her customary thin set lips and they hardly moved for she had no inclination to speak at length. Even Alice "felt" the silence and kept her distance.

When the invitation arrived, she held it in her hand as if it were a burning coal and stared at it, afraid that her mother might see it and that it would start the bitterness and angered outpourings, all over again. Her Mother's face when she was angry and full of rage, was quite ugly and as well as being totally incomprehensible for the purpose of lip reading it was the wild eyes and screwed features that Alice still feared. She decided to take the letter into the garden and sat at a small bench underneath an oak tree, she tore at her gloved hands to remove them and slide the invitation from the ivory envelope. She pulled out a formal invitation on embossed card and stating the desire of the happy couple for her to join them in the wedding ceremony at the Registry Office in Bristol at the beginning of November. Her first instinct was to tear it up, but there was a letter with it as well and Alice found that Bella's character flowed through the words. She had practically begged Alice to attend because she felt sure that no-one else from the family would be there and her own parents were too old and frail to make the trip from America. Several times she addressed her as --- *Dearest Alice.* It was hard to separate the actions of this lovely woman from the idea of them never being a part of the Church, to be denied a marriage in the sight of God. Her mother had called her a wicked, evil woman, but Alice could not see her as any of that. She surmised that it was not really Bella's fault as she was an innocent unaware of the teachings of the Church, but Jack knew. So was it his fault, for not instructing his fiancé? It was all too confusing and Alice was sure she wanted nothing more to do with either of them, yet an hour later she was still sitting re-reading the letter.

Bella had sat at the desk in the window of her room in the guest house, pausing; reflecting upon the woman that was her fiancés sister. There was a calmness and simplicity that surrounded Alice. She did not want to use the word naivety, but it seemed apt in a sense that she had witnessed a person who witnessed much; but lived slightly below the surface of all that surrounded her, a person who noticed the things others had no time for and also it appeared, had a quiet acquiescence and acceptance of her lot in life. Her deafness, it seemed to Bella, meant that Alice was living on a different plane. She liked her eyes, she liked her smile and wanted to get to know her more. Back at home in Boston, she had heard of a family who had put their daughter into a mental institution because she was deaf and dumb. She shuddered to think of Alice in such a place. She hoped she would come to give her blessing to her and Jack, but it didn`t seem likely.

The subject of the wedding was not mentioned, but everyone knew the date was fast approaching. Alice had pretended she didn`t know, if no-one had not mentioned the date, which no-one in her family had done; then she would have no way of knowing anyway; but she had the invitation. She had never told a lie in her life and wondered if it was something she would have to admit in due course in a confessional, but she had decided she was going--- just to get a glimpse of her brother and his new--- what? She was his wife, but would never be called that by her Mother. She knew the teachings, but looking at the eyes of Christ in her picture on her wall, she wondered if He would allow her to be a by-stander.

She took the risk and went, not being too smartly dressed, telling her Mother she was meeting a colleague for coffee in Castle Street and with a pounding heart she caught the bus. The building had a sort of resemblance to a church, but it would be a Protestant church if it were to be one, thought Alice. At first she thought she had got the time wrong and glanced at the clock on a building nearby. Three o`clock, well the service was at quarter to three and she had been told once that these services were short and without any spiritual significance, so she thought she had missed them coming out. She didn`t want to turn around and walk away, because if they did come out she wouldn`t be aware of them. She turned up her collar and waited. Five minutes later the doors opened and she saw them emerge amongst a scattering of rice. She saw the smiles and the waving hands and arms, the hugs of the few friends who had accompanied them, a dozen people in all. Her handsome brother in a dark suit and Bella wearing a simple cream suit, pearls at her throat and her hair with a silk cream band and a single white camellia. She looked radiant. Jack suddenly looked in Alice`s direction and his face fell and then he broke into a smile and waved vigorously, beckoning to her she thought; but realised he wasn`t actually looking at her. She followed his gaze and froze, seeking a tree to hide behind, she saw her Mother was some distance away watching the bridal party. Aileen hadn`t seen Alice, but when she realised that Jack had seen her she turned and walked away. She prayed to God for his eternal soul.

Alice waited until her mother turned the corner and with feet of lead she approached the party, she was embraced, hugged, kissed and swept along to a small reception and found that the meal and the company was very agreeable, not to mention a warming sherry or two.

It was a long time before anyone at home mentioned Jack and Bella again.

Chapter 15

Ireland still held its softness, the greenery and fresh fragrance was the additional welcome that Alice had wanted. Jimmy had suggested she come for a short break at Christmas and although she was torn and felt she should be at home to help there, Aileen seemed keen to encourage her to go. "It will be good for you Alice. You have been looking awful peaky of late, go and fill your lungs with the Old Country" It was the smile that was noted, it had been a long time coming.

The Christmas was a good one with food that could feed an army, with puddings from Jimmy`s wife`s mother and locally produced chickens, hams and bacon and all manner of cakes and pastries. Jimmy seemed happy and was thrilled to see that his sister was an elegant woman. He longed for her to be happy, but wondered if she would ever have a family of her own. She was rather tied to looking after their Father who was becoming even more frail. She needs a life of her own he thought.

The evenings were full of laughter and music and dancing and Alice happily joined in. The jigs and reels were fast and furious making them all giddy, the music not heard, was not needed for her appreciation. Jimmy slipped an arm around his wife`s shoulders and kissed her tenderly on her cheek. "I wish I could do something for Alice, wish I could give her something here to give her a life, what would you think to that?"

"It is something you`ll have to think on, but she would have to have paid work, it can`t be charity now"

"I know, I know, I`ll put my mind to it---- but for now come and dance with me, my fair Irish Queen!" as he spun her round and danced around the barn that had been cleared for the occasion, the violinists and the tambour player whipping the dancers into a frenzy.

In the morning there were several thick heads and the greetings of the night before were muted. The grey mist settled until a watery sun broke through the cloud in the early afternoon and Alice walked alone through the village streets. The shops were shut for the holidays and it seemed everyone was sleeping late that day, but Alice always rose early and was in her element in the country lanes. The two dogs were still fairly young and eager for a walk, but Jimmy felt that they were still too unruly for Alice to walk; so the setters stayed chained in the barn and Alice set off by herself. She could walk for miles, often unaware of the passage of time; just content to be in the open watching the birds or pausing to see a rabbit dive under a bush. She was completely lost in her own world. It was an hour or more before she thought she ought to turn back and head back to Jimmy`s farm. The wind had started to get up and as she walked back into the village a few items bowled around at her feet. The torn page of a poster came fluttering like a monochrome butterfly and wrapped around her feet. She bent to unwind the paper from her ankles and as she did so a face was revealed, crumpled and torn, the image rocked her and she felt goose bumps on her flesh. It was the eyes. The eyes of the one who had stood at her gate, the one who had seen her at the barracks, the one she suspected had given her father a black eye and who she felt sure was involved with the fire. His face was older and more lined, but it was him, a black and white picture of the sandy-haired man. The words and information were torn, his name gone. She shivered and started to read the little that was there; thinking that maybe it was a report of some other wrong doing or a court appearance, but was horrified to see that he was now a prominent political figure. How could that be? It was very confusing and she folded the paper and put in her coat pocket. She would take it and show Jimmy. He might be able to tell her about it.

They were all a little less bleary eyed and were sitting by a welcoming log fire when Alice entered. Jimmy saw how pale she looked.

"What`s wrong? Alice?" but she beckoned for him to come out into the kitchen where the pair were alone. She took the paper and spread it out on the table before him.

"Oh God, no Alice, no. Don`t be putting that there." Hastily he snatched up the paper and rolled it into a ball, then swiftly opened the door to the range and flung it into the flames. It seemed that for a few moments they were both transfixed, watching the paper curl and bend upon itself, before becoming a twist of ashes, memories of other flames in their heads. He put his fingers to his lips and shook his head, his fear was tangible. He snatched up a pencil and a scrap of brown baking paper and with an eye on the door, he wrote.

"Never, never, mention the fire or anything about father to anyone, our secret ok" and upon hearing someone in the passage, he flung that too into the kitchen stove. He hoped that he hadn`t shocked her too much, but he also hoped that she understood the need to keep silent and not to ask questions. His tranquil life depended upon it.

That night he held Erin in his arms and whispered to her what Alice had seen in the paper. "Will she understand that it is troubled times and that she must be quiet and not be giving any judgements, maybe the time isn`t right for her to come here" She said with real concern.

"Maybe, maybe" replied Jimmy, " She might be better off at home, but remember you can take the Irish out of Ireland, but you can't take Ireland out of the Irish--- and she loves this place too, she'll want to be here"

"Did you know too, that Patrick is taking her to the bar tomorrow, how do you think that will fair? he seems gentle enough." Erin told Jimmy.

Patrick was a young man they had come to know recently and he had taken a shine to Alice.

"Does he know she's deaf, he must surely know it?"

"Yes, he does that, he had guessed, but he asked me if he should ask her, I see no harm, so long as she doesn't talk about past events, I don't know him well enough, what do you think?"

"I'll go there too and watch for them both, I think Alice will be shy and it will be difficult for Patrick, I have to also trust someone and I think he is trustworthy--- but I doubt anything can come of this."

Patrick had watched Alice and thought her an attractive woman, with her fair skin, blue eyes and blonde hair. He knew she was deaf but wondered if he could at least be friends with her; maybe it wouldn't matter, maybe she could teach him to spell on his fingers like Jimmy did. He was intrigued by her and thought that the pub would be a good place to go with so many people squeezed into that place and the warm ambiance he thought it would put her at her ease. Alice had walked there with Jimmy, slightly annoyed that her brother wanted to walk with her, but knew that it was his way of giving permission for the meeting. Their mother would not have approved, both knew that. "'Tis common women who frequent the bars." Jimmy had heard it from her lips and Alice had known her mother's feelings on the matter looking scornfully at the women who went to the pub after Sunday Mass and they were mainly accompanied by their men. She felt perhaps she was a common woman. In any case she would have to launder her clothes before she went home because of the cloying cigarette smoke that hung in grey clouds and was now in her hair and clinging to her skirt and cardigan.

Jimmy saw Patrick sitting at a small table by the fire and indicated the table to Alice. Jimmy stayed at the bar and watched as his sister pushed through the crowd of drinkers, mostly men; which made her feel uncomfortable. Patrick patted the vacant seat and she sat down. He smiled at her, she smiled back. He asked her three times what she would like to drink and she could not understand him. All around were faces, mouths opening and closing, silently laughing and smiling. Mouths downing pints or quaffing a small ale, they all felt too close and she felt overwhelmed. They tried again to talk and she realised that Patrick kept looking up and that Jimmy was doing a good mime act to help Patrick with the conversation. She glowered at Jimmy and turned his back on the couple, which left them struggling again. There were a lot of pauses in the flow of dialogue and several times Patrick thought she was upset because her voice rose dramatically. He felt sad because she was a lovely woman, but he was out of his depth and he knew she felt uncomfortable too. The fire was blazing and little room for anyone to sit, so it was no surprise that Alice suddenly felt very hot and fanned her face with her handkerchief. Patrick downed his pint and indicated the door. Alice looked to see if Jimmy was watching, but his great back was turned and he was talking to a fellow drinker. She felt lost, not sure if she should walk outside with this man, but he seemed kind enough. Her heart thumped as he took her elbow and led her outside.

Jimmy did not see their exit. Outside, Patrick lit a cigarette and remembering his manners offered one to Alice which he was surprised she accepted. She smiled a lot and he just wished he could have an easy talk with her. He pointed to his watch and did a sort of mime about walking home. It wasn`t far to Jimmy`s but it gave him time to realise this could go no further. It was a shame but this could never work and he hoped she knew it too. At the gate he bent to kiss her on the cheek.   She reacted by pulling her face back unsure if this would be a kiss on the lips, unsure if that was what she wanted or not. She blushed, but was actually flattered by the brush of his lips on her cheek. "Goodnight Alice" he said and watched as she entered the house. He would not ask her out again. Alice was reeling from the kiss and hoped for more from the friendship but in the cold morning light she knew that her hopes lay with finding someone who shared her deafness, who also lived in her silent world. He had however, taught her that some men are gentlemen.

"I think I should go home now" Alice said the next day to her brother and sister-in-law. She needed to be back at home and to return to work. They both noted how radiant she looked, the Irish air had done her good. Jimmy`s heart went out to her, he couldn`t always be there for her; she was going to have to learn to fend for herself.

It had not gone unnoticed that people seemed less inclined to give the warm Irish welcome to all that they met, strangers were strangers and whilst caps were doffed and an occasional smile given, it seemed to Alice that she noticed a stiffness and a tendency towards mistrust. She was a good reader of body language and things had changed. She knew of the history of the land and had learnt about the separation, but there were still areas of the politics that she did not understand. She wished that Jimmy would explain more to her, but she did not want to upset him and she herself was still upset regarding her friendship with Patrick. At school in Yorkshire she had been drilled by the Nuns regarding chastity and modesty. She knew about Eve`s sin. She had no immoral thoughts because she knew these to be a sin. Her naked body had been covered in the special robe when she bathed, a difficult thing to deal with both practically and emotionally. It meant that her feelings of femininity were mixed up to say the least. She wondered about men and marriage, but decided that she would have to shelve those longings for the moment and still felt that she was very young. Time enough, she thought, time enough. Life seemed full of pieces of a jigsaw that she was having to piece together alone.

At home again she noticed that in her absence her father seemed to have rallied, he was definitely greyer and slower, but he did not seem so frail as in the previous months; he seemed made of stern stuff. It was her mother who seemed more stooped, more prone to headaches, however she insisted on soldiering on unless they became so bad that she reluctantly took to her bed. Aileen had always insisted that one should not grumble about illness and that it was generally idle people who became ill, something her own mother had said often and so it was known that she really was unwell when she took to her bed.

Alice fell back into routine working at the hair salon, helping at home and with the small holding. She attended Mass and became as involved with the church as much as she could. She prayed and kept her daily devotions, wondering about the world and always including prayers for her family. Why was there so much hate in the world? Why couldn`t people see how easy it could be? But she herself avoided walking past the Protestant church at the end of the village, she could never be sure about non-Catholics.

Chapter 16

In the years that passed, it seemed to Alice there were many moments when she came home from work to find her parents and maybe other members of the family, gathered around the wireless. She was ready for their annoyance if she interrupted their listening. She preferred to read her books, detective stories being her favourite especially Miss Marple. The library was a small affair, but it had most of what she enjoyed. On that occasion when she looked up from reading she saw that they all had serious faces, it took a while before someone realised that Alice had no idea what was going on. Her father tried to explain and gave up and wrote down." The King has given up his crown and will marry Wallis Simpson". It seemed to Alice that they received this news with the same shock as James and Bella`s intentions, yet they were all discussing this as if they knew the King personally; or the now ex-King. She had seen pictures of Wallis Simpson in the newspapers and read some of the reports, she did not like her. Alice thought she looked very masculine and harsh and wondered what he saw in her, another case of someone falling in love with the wrong person; or was it that this was the right person, wrong circumstances? She didn`t know and wondered what his brother thought, because he would be King now. They all carried on talking and Alice read her book.

Each night they lowered the gas mantle and lit this for gas light, but Alice still carried an oil lamp to her room each night. The large accumulator, the battery for the wireless, had to be lifted into a neighbour's lorry and taken to the local ironmongers to be charged. It seemed that her mother was in mourning whilst it was away.

One sunny September morning, two years later, the radio gained immense notoriety and became the voice of a nation at war. It seemed strange to Alice that her parents had decided to attend the earlier Mass at eight thirty in the morning and had positively hurried out of the church, everyone seemed anxious and her father had looked very grave in discussions with his male companions. They had stopped to shake hands with the Priest and had then walked briskly home. Once inside the house they had gathered around the radio. It surprised Alice that some friends of her parents had come home too, she knew that they did not have a radio and now they all crowded into their parlour. Alice looked at their faces downcast and serious, she opened her mouth to ask if this was to do with the problem with Mr. Hitler, but once again was shushed, finger to his lips her father turned up the knob that she assumed meant they could hear more clearly. The clock on the mantel said eleven fifteen, Alice noted that twelve minutes went by before anyone spoke. Her mother was wringing her hands again and biting her lip, her father had sunk lower into his chair, she knew that if he could he would have adopted his customary stance by the mantel, but he could still light a pipe. The unnamed friends, who Alice only knew to nod to, were pale and visibly shaken. Her father caught her looking with equal anxiety and spoke so she could lip read.

"It's war Alice, we are at war!"

Alice sneezed and her mother shot her a look and pressed her fingers to her lips. The wireless was alive again and they were all looking very grave. They carried on listening and Alice looked at their pale faces and the woman from across the road was dabbing her eyes. Her father was standing up now and reaching for a purchase on the mantel. "What--- what has happened?" Alice was anxious to know having read the papers. "War," said her mother "It's war" there was no need for any other words. A newspaper a copy from a few days ago lay on a nearby chair and the face of Hitler was visible, looking afresh at his face; Alice studied his eyes and concluded that all evil men had it written on their faces. She felt the weight of this news was so very sad, wondering about the last war; hadn't she read somewhere that it was the war to end all wars. She was 26 years old and yet she suddenly felt so old, so full of worries. After the broadcast that Neville Chamberlain had delivered, there had been a list of instructions about what was expected of people immediately and things that needed to be done to ensure safety of individual homes and public places. Alice hugged her hot cup in her hands and felt that life was about to change again.

That afternoon with the dog at her heels she walked into the village to see people standing around talking or filling sand bags, but it seemed apart from that, like any other sunny September day, summer still shining and hints of autumn on the way. She walked on through the lanes with a cardigan around her shoulders and a head full of thoughts. Two small boys with grubby knees and ruddy cheeks came hurtling towards her laughing and arms outstretched they made like aircraft in a dog fight, their silent rat-a-tat-tats of machine gun fire rattled past, as they dived and swooped each side of her. They seemed happy, she hoped they would not see the real results of such fighting.

Alice protested that her mother was treating her like a child when she insisted that everyone had to have name labels sewn into their clothes, she argued that that was probably just for children and didn't see her mother sewing name labels for her father. It made her immensely happy when their identity papers arrived. She had also read that some children might have to be sent away if towns and cities received bombing. She shivered at the thought of bombing, but also shuddered because she wondered if there was any intention to send her away too. Her mother tried to explain that it was more necessary for Alice to have her name on her person at all times. She along with everyone else received her gas mask, which she constantly had to go back to fetch as she walked out the door to go to work; it hadn't become habit yet. Aileen felt awful when she absent-mindedly handed Alice the ear plugs that had been given out, protection from any imminent blitz. Alice just smiled and handed them back. The black- out curtains were made and the windows criss-crossed with tape to hold them in place in case of bomb blast. A shelter was created in the garden with steps leading down into the basement. She helped her mother carry some hurricane lamps into the shelter along with some packing crates to sit on. It looked very gloomy and felt cold and damp, Liam noticed that when it rained the water trickled down the steps and in under the door. He hoped that being farther out from the big city that they would not need to use it. He couldn't believe that this was happening, the same nations locked in conflict again. Was there such a thing as lasting peace?

For a time it seemed that the war wasn't really happening. The rationing was implemented and clothing coupons, but in the farming communities there was little shortage of milk and eggs. A young lad had come once a week to help Liam create more space in the garden for vegetables. The old man was merely acting in an advisory capacity. As well as chickens, ducks had been introduced and the lad whose name Alice never knew, helped to dig out a small area to serve as a pond for the ducks. That seemed cruel to Alice, why give the ducks hope of a nice life with water to splash in and then take one of them away for the chop? "You eat lamb" was her mother's reply. True. "Life is cruel, Alice, you have to survive!" Alice understood. Sometime after the introduction of the ducks, the young lad stopped coming and Alice assumed he had gone to the army or the navy or some other war effort. Some of the girls her age in the village had gone to work as land girls and there was something in the Church news about ATC's it took a while to find out about that. They all worried about Jack but as far as Alice could tell, he wasn't openly mentioned.

Jimmy and others from Ireland wrote regularly, worrying about the situation and sending a few treats that were unavailable in England. One aunt wrote that she would soon be making her Christmas puddings and that she would be sure and make extra to send to make Christmas special even in dark times. Dark times literally for Alice, in the evenings the lack of street lights made it very difficult for everyone, but it especially scared her. Unable to know who was behind her had always been a problem, and crossing a street was a hazard whether from the danger of a motorised vehicle or a bicycle, but with no street lights it was a hazardous affair. Her balance was not good at the best of times and this didn't help matters, she didn't know that even in well lit circumstances, her inability to walk a straight line had caused people unused to her, to wonder if she had been drinking.

The hair salon saw fewer customers, but they stayed open and it was a warm cosy haven for Alice, doing a job that she loved. The buildings around however bore a constant reminder of the threat they were all under, with sandbags and black outs and shops were shut early. Social life in Castle street had been suspended.

For the first two weeks of the war, all cinemas and theatres were shut and Alice wondered when they would reopen because it was one of her delights to go to the cinema.   Her parents were reliant on the radio, listening avidly for news but more often than not listening to dreary music. Alice did not know any German people, but she worried about what would happen if Hitler arrived in Britain. She wondered what would happen to her as a deaf woman. The training in the village hall for a mock gas attack became a farce with the children not taking it seriously and lots of giggling, Aileen worried that Alice might be out and about and never hear the siren.

Then Emily arrived. Aileen and Liam had objected at first, citing their old age as a reason for objection and that they still had Alice to consider, but as others in their village had been ordered to take evacuees from London, they too had little choice. It seemed that Somerset was deemed a place of refuge. That Saturday afternoon in August 1940, Emily arrived at the station in Midsomer Norton. She was seven years old and clasping her doll, her gas mask and a battered brown leather case; she stood with the other children looking around her with big brown eyes, a label around her neck, like a parcel. She was taken by car to the house and handed over to Liam and Aileen. The poor child was scared and homesick and thought her hosts were old and not particularly welcoming. She had been given a little room at the front of the house and an attempt had been made to make it welcoming. Alice had only been told the day before but put some of her old childhood books on the bed. Her first encounter did not go too well as Emily sucked her thumb and cradled her doll. She did notice that Alice was beaming at her and seemed friendly, but when she spoke her voice was funny and Emily started to cry. Gradually however, Emily realised that she could go to Alice and stroke the dog or go for a walk. Gradually too she learnt to understand what Alice was saying to her and liked to be read too, although the words were flat and without intonation. Emily never let on that she was reading ahead ; it was the company that she craved. They sat together with "Alice in Wonderland" and whilst Alice wrote in her diary, Emily wrote to her parents. The seven year old Emily reminded Alice of herself when her world changed. Alice taught Emily how to finger spell and it meant that the two could keep amused and not hinder Aileen and Liam who were both too old to really be bothered with such a young child. Alice and Emily could face the war together.

Emily watched as she saw Alice on her knees saying her prayers, fingering her rosary; to a child who had no religious upbringing it was all very strange. She looked at the image of Mary and Christ with his bleeding heart. She took comfort in hearing Alice include her name in her prayers. For Alice, she just continued to work and tried not to worry about the war, which still hadn`t had any real impact on her, apart from rationing and having to make do and mend. She wrote endless letters to Jimmy and to her sisters and brothers and worried about Jack. She had not heard from Bella for a while and Jack`s last letter had been sent on via Bella and had been heavily censored. She had no idea where he was or on what vessel. He was in her prayers too.

Aileen came back from the village one day with a leaflet that had been handed out, she placed it on a table in the hall and made sure everyone read it. As a devote Catholic the content pleased her. It read

MORALE ---- HOW YOU CAN PLAY YOUR PART

*FORGET YOURSELF IN HELPING YOUR NEIGHBOURS—THIS CASTS OUT YOUR OWN FEARS AND WORRIES.

*KEEP THE MORAL STANDARD OF THE NATION HIGH--- MAKE A BREAK WITH ALL PERSONAL INDULGENCES, SELFISHNESS AND PRIVATE WARS WHICH UNDERMINE MORALE AND NATIONAL UNITY.

*BE A RUMOUR STOPPER --- ANY PATRIOT SHOOTS RUMOUR DEAD ON SIGHT.

*THE SECRET OF STEADINESS AND INNER STRENGTH IS TO LISTEN TO GOD AND DO WHAT HE SAYS.

*FOREARM YOURSELF BY LISTENING TO GOD EVERY MORNING – THIS GIVES A CLEAR PLAN FOR EACH DAY.

*A BRITISH GENERAL WHO HAS FOUGHT TWO WARS SAID THIS: TO LISTEN TO GOD AND OBEY HIM IS THE HIGHEST FORM OF NATIONAL SERVICE.

This had been printed and distributed by the Morale Re-Armament Society. Aileen bade everyone read this each morning.

Emily sat with Alice each morning and watched her as they ate together, said Grace before meals and then gathered her school things and walked to school holding her hand. When the shy little girl had arrived her skin had been pale and she seemed very thin, now she had a ruddy glow to her cheeks, had more flesh upon her bones and was seen to skip alongside Alice, with her flaxen plaits bouncing on her shoulders. The child missed her parents but had the warmth and love that she needed and she was thriving. She bounced into school and Alice walked on to take her bus to Bristol, it was their daily routine. The weekends were for rambles, helping in the Church, cooking and sewing, writing letters and trying not to get in Aileen`s bad books, especially when August came and school was out.

Emily also liked to listen to the radio, it was the news of the first bombs over London that had Liam reaching over to switch off the set. Emily had heard, wanting to know where in London. The letter from her parents couldn`t arrive soon enough.

Then came the raids on Coventry and Emily wasn`t allowed to go to see the news reels with Alice. The news reels showed shattered homes, but portrayed a nation that would not have it`s spirits shattered. Everywhere were posters encouraging, trying to keep the upper lip stiff and proud, although many lips were trembling.

One evening a month later, a man from the other side of the village came in holding his cap in his hand and with red-rimmed eyes, he told of how his brother had died at a raid at the aircraft factory in Filton. The factory at Filton near Bristol was hit and it seemed that just over seventy people had been killed and over one hundred seriously injured. The shocking events were revealed about the raid that had taken place in broad daylight. He was told to sit down and a glass of sherry placed in his hand, he wiped his tears and said.

"My sister in law saw them coming over but she thought they were ours, they were in a Y shape and she looked up and saw them, but then she saw the German markings--- my brother was in the works---- we think they were running for the shelters---- he didn`t make it---- my sister-in-law says there are bodies still in the shelters---"

He broke off sobbing and Liam comforted him, "There were soldiers too marching up the road and they were machine gunned, eleven are dead, they,--- they are still digging out the bodies----" Emily stood in the doorway and was ashen faced.

"Alice, take Emily to her room." Aileen asked.

Alice was not sure what had been said but could see the distress and didn`t need to be asked twice, but would want details later.

There were no pictures in the local paper, there was nothing on the wireless apparently, but word of mouth had the number of fatalities rising and the shock that the raid was in daylight. Two days later another attempted raid on the factory was met by RAF Hurricanes and there were no more casualties

It was all too close to home.

The evenings were darker and colder and as autumn became winter Alice and Emily started to prepare for Christmas it was only nearing the end of November, but Emily was excited and wondering if she would be able to go home to her parents, no-one knew if that was possible but they would at least start to make Christmas cards with brown paper and things she had gathered from the woods, sycamore wings and acorn cups. She was already painting fir cones. Alice had taken Emily on the bus to see Castle Street, it was unlikely the shops would have the same Christmas displays of past years and the shops were not open late, the blackout and curfew had put paid to that, not that anyone wanted to be out and about anyway---. The shops did still have a fascination with or without their colourful displays, the buildings themselves were interesting and in daylight the street still bustled with the trams and commuters. Emily had wanted some scarlet ribbons, but these were hard to come by, so that evening when they returned home, Alice had taken some old material from an old scarf and cut a piece into a length and cutting it in half, had two red ribbons for Emily. Make do and mend.

The next morning was the same as any other and Emily skipped to school with red ribbons in her plaits, she kissed Alice on the cheek as Alice walked on to wait for her bus to take her to Bristol and to her work in the hair salon. She blew on her hands as she waited for the bus, pulling on her gloves and stamping her feet in the cold November air. She waited and waited, there was no sign of the bus. There was little sign of any traffic either, not that there was ever a great deal. She checked her watch, she had been waiting for a good forty minutes and was getting colder and colder by the minute. There was nothing for it she decided, she would have to walk, at least she could keep warm by walking and Alice never minded walking. It did surprise her however that no-one else was waiting for the bus. The walk to Bristol from Midsomer Norton took her a good few hours, but she kept walking with a rising panic; as in the distance she saw black smoke rising and the sky line was rosy. As she walked into Bristol she could not believe the scene that she witnessed. The twisted metal and debris from the shattered buildings, the bridge across one part of the river was gone; a bus lay on its side. Historic buildings were gone, the church was minus its` roof; glass and rubble everywhere. Everything was smouldering or being doused by water hoses. People were wandering about aimlessly, some picked through the rubble looking for possessions, some sported make-shift bandages. Pieces of masonry hung precariously from buildings. Alice walked on as if in a dream, her silent footsteps crunching the glass under foot. Her face streamed with tears as she walked on and rounded the corner into what should have been Wine Street,-----gone! Walking on into what should have been her beloved castle Street---gone!

The beautiful shops were gone, a pile of smouldering rubble where Woolworth`s should have been, the road littered with charred timbers and harrowingly, she saw shoes and hats and sheets that she presumed covered bodies. The acrid smell of smoke filled her lungs. So much destruction and she didn`t know if the siren still sounded, was the blitz still happening? She looked at the sky and surmised that it was over but

81

walked on full of fear and dread. She tried to locate the hair salon and found her way barred by a heap of rubble and a building sliced open like the front of a dolls' house with the doors removed, each floor and room visible, the curtains and tattered wallpaper blowing in the breeze. As she stood and stared, she jumped violently as an arm shot out and grabbed her. A woman air raid warden with her ARP helmet, had seen her and pulled her away from the building as a piece of masonry crashed to the ground. The woman's mouth screamed words from a grey ash covered face. She seemed angry, shouting; but when she must have realised that Alice was deaf; her arm went around her and they walked back towards an area that seemed less likely to fall upon them both. " Go home!" she mouthed " Go home, it's not safe here!" It made no use trying to protest and pointing to where the salon should have been, the female warden was tired having been on watch all night and refusing to go off duty; she had seen too much death and destruction to be patient any longer. "Turn around!" she yelled " Go home!"

As if in a trance, Alice turned and picked her way through the rubble and started walking the several hours home again. Her heart felt as if it had been torn from her, her breathing came in rasps and her steps faltered as she made her way over the uneven surfaces; frightened that she might encounter a body or what if a raid started again? She stumbled and fell in her panic, breaking her watch face. She knew it was just her watch and in the scheme of things it was nothing, but Jimmy had given her that watch and looking around she wept. The smell of burning was in her nostrils, taking her back to another place, but this time the evil had fallen from the skies and in so doing had destroyed her world --- once more.

The journey home was long but she didn't really remember it, she just concentrated on putting one foot in front of the other and she got home half walking, half stumbling. It became dark as the City became country. Her small torch had a piece of tissue paper to diffuse its beam as were the regulations, so it was next to useless in helping her way. The brambles that she loved to raid for blackberries, became her enemy as they tore at her coat and stockings. She had no idea how she managed to find her way back, but she did and had never been more grateful to sink into her bed.

Aileen had worried all day, having heard from neighbours, who in turn had heard via the village grapevine, everyone seemed stunned, shocked beyond belief. She had hugged Alice when she returned torn and bleeding slightly. Alice herself had little voice and what there was came quickly and full of panic. The doctor was called and he administered a sedative. It was Aileen who sat and held her hand, but when Alice woke in the morning; it was Emily who stroked her face and flung herself on top of Alice. Aileen watched silently from outside of the bedroom and turned and walked slowly with her aged body, negotiating the stairs to reach the kitchen.

The days that followed were long dark days, because no-one was able to tell Alice if her colleagues had been killed. It seemed likely that they would be alive as the raid had started in the evening and the salon had been closed. The shops had not opened late since the out-break of the war, but gradually they learnt that over a hundred people had lost their lives that night and people started to relate their grisly tales. Two weeks later there was another raid on Bristol and the start of advent was marked by more deaths.

It was a cold winter day when the Duke of Kent came to visit Bristol, to see for himself the damage. A friend of Aileen had got hold of a copy of "The Evening World" and there was a photo of him in Castle Street, or what was left of it.

"Why are those women giving him sausages?" asked Emily. It was a valid question because indeed there were women standing in the remains of the street, either side of the Duke, smiling, handling sausages.

"The Lord himself knows," replied Aileen puzzling over the image "—and why in Heaven`s name are they all smiling so?"

" ---- Ah--- sausages!" said Liam making Emily jump and suppress a giggle. "Sausages, I am sure the Duke of Kent was wondering when he would eat again?"

Jimmy wrote to say that they had only heard on the radio that "--- a town in the West of England, had suffered some casualties,"

"Well that`s alright then." Said Aileen with a sardonic tone holding his letter out to Liam, "We`ll be sure and let the Emerald Isle know when we are really under attack!"

The postal service was heavily disrupted, but eventually a letter arrived for Alice from her employer. She was sorry to inform her of the loss of the salon, although she assumed that Alice would have realised this--- everyone was safe and well, thankfully; but she had found out that two of the waitresses that Alice had been on nodding terms with at the tea rooms; had both been killed. There was a personal thanks to Alice for all her service and hard work and an assurance that if in the future, new premises were purchased, then Alice would be notified. Alice faced the realisation that it was not likely to be any time soon.

In the village, Emily attended school at the Methodist hall, which did not please Aileen and Liam at all, but it was where most of the evacuees were receiving classes and it was not a decision that they could influence. It didn`t go down too well when Emily had written in her letter to her parents about attending the Catholic church with Alice. Her parents had no religious convictions, but would probably have answered C of E if questioned on the subject, they had no problems with the Methodists, but Emily's father held the view that his daughter was being silently converted to Catholicism. "Over my dead body!" he had said to his wife. He had unfortunately vented his spleen in a letter to Liam on the subject, Emily had read the letter by mistake when she saw her father's handwriting. She hadn't wanted to question her elderly hosts as they still intimidated her slightly, so she made the mistake of questioning Alice.

"Do Catholics usually have two left feet?" she pointed to her left foot to emphasise the question. Alice thought she had lip read the bit about the left foot, but still asked her to repeat what she was saying.

"Well what are Left Footers? My father says I am not to become a Left Footer. If I go to your Church will something happen to my right foot?" Emily was curious. So was Alice, she'd never encountered the term before, but assured Emily that her two feet were fine the way they were! Alice soon found out it was not a kind phrase for a Catholic to be called, as Liam shouted after her and ranted and raved. Liam was all for sending Emily back to London. It fell to Aileen to diffuse the situation.

"Liam will you behave!, the child's father is ignorant, that he is and I won't tolerate his insults, but the child is innocent and we have her here, it is the way of things. Let all just be, please!"

So nothing more was said and the days of the war continued with the rationing, more raids in London and sleepless nights in the shelters when there were false alarms and when nearby Radstock got hit. Then came the catalyst that caused Emily to go back to London.

The school crocodile was marching up the high street, their teacher to the fore and Emily and her new best friend to the rear. They were going to the library and Emily who had caught the bug for reading was bobbing up and down, her plaits once again dancing on her shoulders. There was no warning, no siren, the leaden sky had been empty one moment and the next a German reconnaissance aircraft came screaming out of the skies. The lone aircraft screamed down the high street, machine gun fire rattling off the pavements and public railings. The screaming children dived for cover and were pulled into open doorways, anywhere that afforded cover. It lasted a few moments and then he was gone. The terrified children and their teacher picked themselves up, looked around to find that miraculously no-one was hurt, save for a few bruises and cuts from their dives to the ground. Emily's father forgot about his concerns about the Left Footers, but decided that all in all he would rather Emily returned to take her chances with them in London. So there was another tearful parting, but the little girl never forgot the kind lady who spoke funny; but who had the broadest grin she had ever know

Chapter 17

The posh shiny black car was parked outside of the house as Alice strolled up the street. It didn't belong to anyone that she knew and it seemed very grand. She entered the house with a sense of curiosity and thought that her mother would probably have the best china out and be refining her airs and graces, as she was convinced that it was someone of high standing, her mother liked to be seen with such people. The atmosphere inside however did not match her expectations. The priest stood in the front parlour with his arm around Aileen, Liam was standing. It was the familiar scene again, father with his pipe not looking at mother.

"What's happened? What's wrong?" Alice felt the black despair and utter misery that seemed to hang in the room. Her parents said nothing. Slowly she realised that this priest was her brother, she hadn't seen him for so long and he had aged, he was so much older than her anyway. How much older? She wasn't sure, she couldn't remember but he was here and something was very wrong. It always was bad news she felt, when someone made you sit down. It was in her head however, before he confirmed it. It had crept into her mind and crawled up her spine, sending shivers of dread, hoping that she was wrong. Jack.

He said it. "Alice, Jack is dead."

"How much more?---- how much more? ----!" Aileen was broken. Her husband never turned away from the wall. Their son was the Priest and he held them, saying the words of comfort that he must have said to many; but finding it so hard now with his own family. He did not know how to communicate with Alice. He tried and found that he could only do what most people do when they seek to comfort another, the hand on her shoulder, the pat of her hand. It was a long time before anyone realised that Alice did not know the circumstances. It was a torpedo, was all she could gather. His ship was gone. She never fully got all the details. It was enough. There were more dark days, more mourning, more wearing of dark clothes; a house that had a dark atmosphere and the waiting for the funeral. A casualty of war they said. It was strange to see her brother conduct the service, to see him stand at the door and shake the hands of the mourners and here was everyone from Ireland. There is nothing like a funeral to gather a family together. Alice watched as Bella sat in her black dress and veiled hat, gloved hand to her face. So gaunt and pale and supported by her friends, none of her family were there, too frail to travel. It was with disbelief that Alice saw her mother pass by the end of the pew and stopped as she drew level with Bella, she reached out and with her own gloved hand she patted Bella on the shoulder. She never looked back and serenely walked out of the church helped by her husband. It was hard for everyone to see Tom there. Tom who looked less like his twin as the years progressed, but never the less had his likeness, his gait his mannerisms and Alice didn`t know it, but he had a similar voice. His toast to his departed brother, when they gathered for the wake, had made some gasp; because of the likeness. There were those that also gasped when Tom walked over to Bella and placed his arms around her. He cared for her because she had been his brother`s wife and as he said to his mother, "Her heart is broken, like ours, she needs our care and I thought even you Mama, would see that too." Aileen felt her own loss like a creature that was eating her from the inside out, she recognised that Bella too was hurting, but had been concerned that Tom was too supportive of this woman. No-one except the priest tried to comfort Alice.

It seemed all too soon family were leaving again, dead, buried, gone. "Dead buried, gone!" Alice said this to herself, but prayed, knowing Jack was a good man and hoping that he had gone to be with all those who had gone before. She prayed for his soul and asked her brother to say a mass for him when he returned to his parish. Her faith was strong, her love of God was fore most in all she did, but sometimes she wondered," why? Why all this suffering?" She wrote this on paper and asked her brother. He wrote back "Dearest Alice, God alone has all the answers, He loves us all, have faith. He loves you" but sometimes He seemed so far away.

In the inky blackness, the gentle motion of the tides lulled her, the full moon shining on the surface of the water. She watched as the moons reflection danced in broken shards, trying to catch the image with her fingers. She realised that she was drifting holding on to a piece of wood, a splinter from a crate or some such thing. Suddenly the sea became a maelstrom foaming black and inky waves tossed her about and she fell into the boiling sea. She felt herself falling slowly through the water and her mouth opened to scream, but she couldn`t , she couldn`t speak and she couldn`t hear. Her hands scrabbled frantically in the water and she panicked as she saw bodies float past her, all with staring eyes and gaping mouths. It was then that she saw Jack as she broke the surface, gasping for air. Her arms found strength and she tried to swim towards him, but she remembered that she couldn`t swim. She panicked again and saw him floating away, he was trying to reach out to her but she couldn`t move and she felt herself sinking lower and lower into the sea. She thought she heard him call her name, but then she remembered she didn`t know what that sounded like. The blackness swallowed her up.

Alice woke with a deep dread, clutching her sheets and realising that she had been dreaming. She had not had such nightmares for a long time. It used to be fire, now she was dreaming about water. It was true that she couldn`t swim. She had never had any lessons and she had always been so full of cold as a child that when the boys splashed about, she had either watched from the banks or in summer waded into the cold water. In the lakes in Ireland she had been wary of the weeds and the undertow. She felt her heart beat fast at the thought of Jack in the water.

It took Bella six months. Six months in which she knew that she could not live without Tom and Tom felt the same way about her. He was scared about telling the family and then decided one day "To hell with them all--- I am damned anyway!" and wrote his letter. Alice had already received hers from Bella. She turned it over and over as if to find writing that had previously been invisible, something that would make easier reading. Alice wanted to think that it could be alright, that it was somehow comforting to think of the two of them being supportive of each other. But it was marriage that they were talking about and Aileen`s sister wrote on her feelings on that subject, their parents had died some time ago and she had become the matriarch, the one feeding Aileen with all her thoughts, instructed Aileen that the woman was pure evil and wickedness personified. Aileen showed the letter to Alice, in the hopes that Alice would understand the family view. It only sent Alice searching for her dictionary to find out what a "Trollop" was. She wasn`t sure that it was Bella. So, like Jack, Tom echoed his twin in being shut out from the family, but Bella kept her heart open to Alice, and Alice never stopped liking and admiring her; although it confused her terribly.

Chapter 18

The war years continued and they learnt to live within their means, it made Alice value what she had. Even as a child in Ireland, there had been the philosophy of "count your blessings," of "eat what `s on your plate" and be grateful. She lived out her life with the "make do and mend" attitude, she hated waste, she had no real hankering after things. She was not a bitter individual, she had a way of seeing things in a positive light and despite her sometimes wondering why she had been left by her mother, when they left for England, she still loved her and held her family with high regard.

She was fond of the cinema and needed it more than ever to give her the information of all the news. It also gave her so much entertainment and a way to view the world. So she viewed the major events of the war with the coverage provided by Pathe Newreels and lost herself in the films of the time.

When finally the war ended the partying seemed to go on for days. Alice had been baking and making bunting and making sandwiches and had helped to decorate the church hall. There were parties in neighbouring streets and everyone wore their best clothes or fancy dress. It was strange to see tables in the streets and families all eating together. There was a lot of dancing and singing and Alice watched as almost everyone had huge smiling faces. Children were running up the street with paper hats and streamers and everyone was hugging someone and Alice joined in the dancing `till her feet ached. It was a celebration of victory in Europe, a celebration of the courage of the armed forces, but for the civilians who had lived through it all; who had lost loved ones; it was a very poignant party.

When the partying was over, there were those in the church who took to speculating about Alice, she was fast becoming the spinster of the parish, with many of the young women having been "snapped up". Aileen was not unaware of the gossiping and wondered herself about her daughter`s future.

With the war over, it still took a long time to start clawing back some normality. Rationing still went on and the landscapes bore constant reminders of what had been lost. Alice was still cutting hair for people in the village and thinking about the idea of going to be with Jimmy and setting up her salon. She was desperately trying to put some money aside, but having to help with finances at home, was making that difficult.

In the years that followed, the house had the installation of electricity and they no longer used the pump in the garden to get their water. It was all becoming very modern. There were more cars on the road and it seemed that people were trying their level best to "Carry on". Her savings grew hoping that there would come a good time to think about her own salon in Ireland.

She had friends, one being a woman who was a fair few years older than her and her husband who had failing sight. Edie herself was hard of hearing, but lived close by and was glad to share her evenings with Alice. They would sit and discuss their lives and Edie had also had a hard time at a boarding school, but her hearing problems had come later. She wore her hearing aids when she felt social events necessitated them, but tried to explain to Alice that they were not a miracle cure. She explained to her, that her hearing was limited and that her aids often "whistled", a concept Alice couldn`t understand. Edie also explained that they amplified all the sound she didn`t want amplified, the background chatter, the clink of tea cups and the rattle of saucers; but she stopped the conversation when she realised that it meant nothing to this young woman. She took a different tack and stated that it was amazing that they had been given to her "free" under the new welfare system. Alice wondered if she could get some.

"You should come with me to the new Deaf club in Bristol---"

Edie was so thrilled to be able to have relatively easy conversations between the pair, she had learnt lip reading and she spoke clearly and the conversation mainly flowed; with a few stalls.

"Where in Bristol and what day?"

"The club is near the old Tramway company, not far from the theatre, ---- I go there on Tuesday evenings, why don`t you come? We can get the bus together,---- it`s a friendly group with people of your age, not all oldies like me. There`s games to play and we have outings and people there to help with any problems we have---- oh do come---- I think you should--- go on---say you`ll come?"

"Yes, alright, I`ll come."

Before the first visit to the club, Alice decided to visit her doctor to ask about the free hearing aids. The GP had known her and the family for years and thought Alice was a very strong character, he liked her and could see that she had a very happy personality; so it pained him to see her face crumple. He had learnt to speak with her.

" I am sorry Alice, but I don't think there is any use in you trying the aids. They only work by making any hearing that you have, much louder. We have done tests before and we know that you have no hearing,---- maybe in the future there will be something that can help, but I am not going to recommend these for you---- you would only be more upset than you are now---"

She tried to take it in but couldn't understand the grades of hearing loss.

"----- besides I have been told that some people give them back,----so much silence and they can't take the sudden noise----" he suddenly realised his insensitivity and was floundering in the conversation----- "like the man who can suddenly hear his nagging wife!"

She didn't laugh, but a smile for his attempts at levity, crept onto her face. It was another of life's disappointments.

The club however was not a disappointment. She walked in to a room at the top of a flight of stairs and found a group of people all talking and laughing. Edie made the introductions. A group of about twenty individuals were sitting playing cards, some playing snooker, some just chatting and smoking. There was a small bar and it wasn't long before Alice, Edie and her husband Ted sat at a table and joined in the game of cards, or at least the two women did. Ted had joked with his friends that they were a right pair, "I'm her ears and she's my eyes"

It was so heart-warming to see these people enjoying a social occasion, without having to apologise for any misunderstandings of communication. Most people seemed to be lip reading each other, a few were using signs to validate the words they were saying, a few were using sign language completely and signing very fast, Alice wasn't one of those who used signing as her main form of communication. She looked around the room and saw a group of young men playing another game of cards. They all seemed to be enjoying themselves and it didn't look like a serious game as in the gangster films she had seen. They were wreathed in cigarette smoke and laughed jovially clapping each other on the back when someone seemed to have had a lucky hand. She watched as they quaffed their pints of beer. She had not blushed in a long time, but she did when she noticed the eyes of one of the men peering at her over the top of his glass. He had seen her looking and raised his glass to her and smiled. She smiled back and suddenly found that Edie was patting her arm.

"Alice, it's your turn, Alice!"

Her head swivelled round again, but there was a warm glow creeping across her neck and face as she found it hard to stop thinking about the man behind her. He had dark hair that was slicked to one side and cut in the way of some of her screen idles. He was no Cary Grant but he was interesting. At the end of the evening, when they had finished discussing the forthcoming events and cleared away the tables, he walked over and spoke to the group.

"Hello Edie, Ted, --are you going to introduce me to your friend?"

"Oh, Joe--- sorry---- this is Alice. Alice let me introduce Joe"

"Hello"

"It`s nice to meet you, I hope you will come again next week, we`re a friendly group and we don`t bite!"

He was walking in the same direction as their little group, towards their bus stop so he tagged along. He was, thought Alice, a charming man and she was sorry when her bus arrived. It didn`t go unnoticed that as the single-decker country bus pulled away, Joe could be seen waving and finished this off by a cheeky blowing of a kiss and for Alice who would not normally have thought that was a bit too forward, she felt the blush rising again. It felt very pleasurable.

Tuesday evenings couldn`t come around quick enough. Here was a man who engaged her in such a charming way. He held her gaze and smiled so much and said such witty things that made her laugh and the people around him found him funny too; but not in a crude way. He wasn`t a show off, he just seemed well, as she said to Edie " He seems so very gentle, a kind gentle man"

"Yes, he is. I am glad you are friends"

They started meeting up on Saturday afternoons and finding a cafe or strolling by the river, they were soon arm in arm. They found a little cafe and sat together but it occurred to Alice that he was self-conscious and so they left to find a bench in the park. He explained that he mainly lip read and like her, used finger spelling for back up. "I am never sure if I am shouting" he said, "I can see people looking sometimes, or it`s when I finger spell, they look then too, I hope then the penny drops---- oh he is deaf" He held her hand and looking serious he continued, "Ours is the hidden disability, you and I don`t have a wheelchair or a dog and a white stick--- it`s difficult isn`t it?"

But he insisted he didn`t want sympathy and with her nodding in agreement he asked her about herself. She told him where she lived, but was keen to add "I was born in Ireland"

"Oh, that`s interesting, tell me about your life there."

She told him about her family and how she came to be deaf, the fire, all about being left and her school in Yorkshire. She told him about Jack and she talked about the war. When she finished, he pulled her hand to his lips and kissed it.

"Oh I am so sorry---- so sorry. You poor thing. You have had a hard time Alice."

He was amazed at how calm she was, how very elegant and well groomed, how her smile captivated him and her eyes held so much life, when so much seemed to have conspired against making those eyes shine.

"What about you?" she asked "Were you born deaf?"

"No" he drew on his cigarette and let out the smoke slowly, carefully avoiding blowing into her face, "No I went deaf in the war"

"Oh"

"I left school and thought of nothing else except going to sea, my father told me tales about his father and the sea and I read about the sea. My grandfather was a sailor who sailed around the Horn and sometimes climbed the rigging in mountainous seas or freezing conditions, I loved those tales of the Seas, all boys' own adventures, felt that it was in my blood. So I went away--- they didn't like it---mother and father--- no they didn't want me to go. I was in the Merchant Navy---- I did a lot of fetching and carrying---- I was just desperate to be at sea----. The ship got hit and I felt the blast and my ear was bleeding. There were men in the sea and a lot of fire."

"Fire and water" thought Alice and was back in the inky black water.

On seeing her sad face he added "Oh I was one of the lucky ones, ---" and his words trailed off. He lifted his head and with a mock laugh continued "Then I had an operation on the ear, but they made a mistake and got the wrong ear, ---my good ear---- and so -----well---- here I am"

Over the years whenever people asked, Alice could never supply the details, because like many elements of her life, the details either hadn't been supplied or she hadn't thought to ask and so it was just the bare bones of the incident that was recalled. There was a fire. The ship got hit.

It seemed that because he had only relatively recently become deaf, Joe still retained the memories of sound. He told her that he could hum the tunes to all of the Glen Miller songs, a fact that she could not verify. He did however have a game that could be verified by his hearing friends as they met in the local pub. Joe would watch some of the drinkers at the bar and then watching some of the conversations he would turn to his hearing friends and say "I think the man with the fair hair is Scottish"

"Yes Joe! You're right! Go on do someone else"

And he would proceed to spot the Geordie or the Welshman, simply by looking at the lip patterns; he was good. Alice told him that she knew that the dog said woof, the cow said moo etc, but they both knew she had no idea what that sounded like.

Their friendship blossomed and she had great pleasure in telling her parents that she was "stepping out" with a man she had met at the Deaf centre. Aileen let it pass for a week or two before the interrogations.

"Is he a Catholic?"

"I don`t know---I don`t think so"

"You must ask him and if he isn`t, then he must attend instruction, he must be Catholic---do you understand now----he isn`t divorced now is he?"

"No!"

"Well be sure to find out about his religion and where does he work?"

"He was a mechanic, he worked with cars, now he makes window frames"

There was an exchange of looks and a sniff of disapproval.

"He`s not a teacher or a lawyer then?"

"No."

" He doesn`t sound as if he has good prospects, what area of Bristol?"

It wasn`t going very well, even though her parents were elderly and frail, her mother`s mind was still sharp and enquiring.

Liam was pleased, if not concerned for his daughter. He genuinely hoped she would be happy. There was the dilemma of their both being deaf, he had hoped that she would find some hearing man to be her husband. Would they cope together? Then he worried about their finances. This man was hardly likely to earn a great deal of money.

Joe answered her questions and didn`t know what he was really, christened in the local parish church, but not a regular attendee, high days and holy days, Christmas, Easter the like.

"-----nothing really C of E I suppose"

"Oh"

Alice suddenly blushed again, because what did it matter what he was, it only mattered if they were to marry and suddenly she quite liked the idea of both.

When he did ask her to marry him, she was over the moon, head over heels.

He had taken to writing letters to her during the week and they were always filled with such sweet sentiments, such outpourings of affection and she would write back telling him of the things she had done and saying how much she looked forward to their next rendezvous. She loved that they both loved books, her with her love of detective novels and he with his novels about the sea, they both loved the cinema and laughed at "Laurel and Hardy", they loved Bob Hope and Bing Crosby. Joe even confessed he was in love with Dorothy Lamour.

So it was easy to say "yes!"

Joe's family had misgivings too, how would he cope with a deaf wife? Life was hard enough for him as it was. They were still adjusting to their son being deaf and had not thought about whether or not his wife would be hearing or not. They were learning how to enunciate each word silently and how to finger spell in BSL, British Sign Language.

Then came the second bombshell, he would have to become a Catholic. He didn't seem to object, it must be love. His mother had heard talk in their small area of Bristol, The Shire. "Hadn't he been in love with a local girl? Weren't they engaged? Didn't she dump him when he went deaf?" If that were true she didn't know about any engagement. It was true that some of his friends had abandoned him, afraid of how to approach him, but Joe himself wanted to try to be the same as possible, go to the same pub, meet with the same people. He also made the decision to attend the "Hard of hearing" group at the Deaf Club because he wanted to keep using his voice and didn't want to be part of the community that relied totally on signing. There were other groups on other nights where they were all fluently communicating in silent signs. He wanted to try and carry on being able to rely on lip reading and not ostracising his hearing mates.

His parents met her and he met hers. They thought Alice a very elegant charming woman and they thought Joe was smart and respectable, although clearly he was ill at ease with them and communication was stilted. It was difficult to get to know them fully. Both parties hoped for the best.

Joe and Alice were in love and couldn't really care, they just knew it was wonderful and when the day came it was all that Alice had dreamed of. She had given Joe a bit of a start before the wedding; when she had produced her birth certificate. He had had no idea. She was thirteen years older than him! He had realised that neither of them were young bride and groom, but he hadn't thought the difference so great. He told no-one, it didn't matter. So what if he was twenty seven and she was forty? It was just a number. She didn't seem to see that it mattered.

She chose to wear a cream suit, thinking that a veil and full dress was not right as she knew she wasn't a young bride, but it was elegant and fetching and he was handsome and dashing.

They went to Ireland for their honeymoon and Jimmy loved Joe and all the family were happy for the couple. Joe loved the fresh air and the clean greenness of it all, they walked and she showed him the places she loved. He saw the bee hives and the uncle who produced honey as well as champion grey hounds and setters. Joe could see why this beautiful Irish girl was in love with her Irish roots.

Their friends in the Deaf Club had helped them to find a flat in Bristol and although it was small, it was homely and they could just afford it. Alice was working again at a new salon but with her old colleagues. She was bursting with happiness.

Joe was a loving husband, tender with Alice who knew so little of the ways of men. It angered him that her mother and sisters seemed to have left her to flounder in society and God love her, she mostly sailed on by. In those first years of marriage she started knitting bootees twice, only to find that the pains came and the dreadful realisation that she was losing another child. Joe didn't know how to fully console her. It seemed that the one thing she longed for was being denied her. She went to her Church and prayed and Joe wished he could fully support her too in her faith, but although he had converted to Catholicism, he left his options open. When she realised again that she was pregnant, she was cautious and waited until she felt the strong kicks of the child inside her before she took up her knitting again. She was so excited, so anxious, so wanting to do this, to be a mother. The ante natal classes were difficult to understand and the midwife talked so fast, so she wasn't sure what to expect. She had read that it was painful, she had seen women in films with the midwife and the boiling water and then the woman in her full make up and best bed jacket, receiving a bonny child. When it started in earnest for her, she was terrified and had never experienced anything like it. Her breathing was out of control and it was difficult for the midwife to get her to understand what she was saying. So in 1955 when men were normally pacing up and down in the corridors, Joe was hurried into a gown and mask and asked to come and hold his wife's hand and to help her with her breathing. He did have to leave before the birth however, some things would have to wait a few decades. When asked after the healthy boy was delivered, she said she hadn't realised it was Joe, she just thought it was a doctor.

She named him James and called him Jimmy. She just held him and watched him, watched him and held him. The traumas of his birth behind her, he was perfect. His cradle swung beside her bed in their little flat, if he cried the cradle rocked and banged her bed and she knew he was crying. She counted his toes and fingers, she stroked his blond hair, she smelt the newness of him and cried. Joe could hold her, put his arms around her, could kiss her; but nothing could capture the feeling of utter joy of holding her baby. Three years later, Alice gave birth to another son after more pain of miscarriages, her happiness just intensified.

Her path in life had been so hard so full of stones, so silent, but now she had made it, she had come so far.

Chapter 19

1995   Nursing home somewhere in Ireland.

"Have you had enough of watching the television now, Donal?"

The woman in the checked nylon overall stood in front of him with that look she always had, a look that made him feel like a child.

She continued "Are you alright there, shall I fetch you another cup of tea?" He brushed her away with his good hand and nodded his head indicating a decline of her offer. He tried to remember how long he had been in this home, with its high ceilings and decorative mouldings and Victorian fireplaces. As homes went it wasn`t too bad he thought, having visited several when his son took him around on a grand tour; he knew his son was paying a pretty penny for him, yet despite being one of the "better" establishments, the smell of cabbage and stale urine lingered. He had had enough of television and closed his eyes hoping that they would not try to persuade him to participate in another soul destroying round of bingo.

He had ended up in need of care when he had a stroke several months ago and his whole world imploded. He had been through many things in his long life, had witnessed things that tore out his heart and those of others, but he could not reconcile himself to this life of humiliation. His mind was still fairly active, not bad for a man of ninety-seven; he was allowed the odd difficulty with recollecting faces, but it was the lack of speech, the lack of feeling in his legs and left arm that drew him inward and miserable. His slack jawed appearance was one he could not bear to look at in the mirror in his room. When Mavis the nurse who helped him to dress each morning had finished the ordeal of hoisting him into the bath and then hoisting him out using the sling and electronic device, she always ended the ritual when he was dressed and sitting in his chair again, with a hearty,

"Well now, aren`t you the handsome one"

He hated it, hated that he was now like a child, hated that his once head of red hair was gone and a liver spotted bald pate was left to him. The skin on his hands was parchment thin and liver spotted too.

The staff all mainly middle aged women in the same blue and white checked overalls busied themselves with tea trays around the other residents who were seated in various high back chairs in a semi-circle facing the large television mounted on a metal bracket on the wall. They were all excited and chattered amongst each other and addressed the residents.

"Well now, wasn`t that exciting to be seeing the American President, Mr Clinton himself up in Belfast, so he was"

Donal had been thinking about that fact, he had watched the President at the City hall in Belfast. Donal might not be able to talk coherently but with his hearing aids he had heard Bill Clinton say "The people want peace, the people will have peace"

Maybe he thought, maybe, but in his heart there were too many wounds, too many scars that made him bitter and prejudiced. His sons had carried that bitterness and it had cost him his political campaign. It had also cost him in tears and standing beside grave sides in the bitter cold wind as the tears streamed down his face. He was part of the Irish troubles. His grandchildren carried the bitterness into their bloodline, but it was the one who had stood before him three years ago and renounced any involvement with his father`s activities. He told his Grandfather, that he was done with the shadows of the troubles, living in fear and he would not be a party to the scheming and plotting and that he was sick of the blood that was spilled on Irish soil. He said that he was moving to London and taking his family away to still be Irish, but to allow his children to grow up proud and not ashamed of their heritage. It wounded Donal when his grandson, turned his back on him and raged that he hated the family and never wanted to be a part of it any longer. Paul was the radical, the one who had found religion. It broke his mother`s heart that he had broken with the Catholic faith and belonged to some sort of cult, a protestant gathering. "Shame on you!" she had yelled.

"At least I don`t kill in the name of religion" He had retorted the day he left for London.

That evening Donal`s son arrived, Paul`s father. He paced the room where his father sat in a chair by his bed, the flaps of the sling underneath him like a parachute and ready for hoisting. He wished he was bailing out of an aeroplane and plunging to his death. His son was pale and holding back his tears as he placed his hand upon his father`s shoulder.

"it`s bad news Dada, it is Megan Paul`s daughter... your great granddaughter.. She, she is in the hospital in London.. She has been so ill with a fever to her brain..." He sobbed and sat down in a chair opposite his father, ruffling his own mop of sandy hair.

"She was in a coma for three days and then when she woke they have found that she can`t hear... nothing! She can`t hear... it isn`t going to be like you with your hearing aids... she has fits and she won`t ever hear again, so they are saying.... Oh Dada... poor mite. Oh our sweet little Megan... not to hear anything!"

Donal listened and suddenly stared wildly into the space before him, he remembered a pair of crystal blue eyes and a girl with curly blonde hair; he remembered calling her names and taunting her.... She was the only deaf child he had known... and suddenly his body became wracked with sobs, he bent double in his chair beating the air with his fists. His son bent to hug and comfort his father...

"Oh Dada, Dada I am sorry, It is alright, it is alright..." and he hugged his father thinking that his grief was directed solely towards Megan. But as Donal`s tears fell, he smelt the smoke in his nostrils and heard the crackle of flames as he recounted throwing the hurricane lamp and the smell of kerosene that had been doused in the barn. He remembered the whinnying of horses and the orange blaze that engulfed everything. He remembered the fights with the military personnel and the punches that were swung. He had remembered many times when flames and bullets and blood had mingled and yet until now he had not remembered the piercing eyes of the little deaf girl. If she had lived or died, she was with him now and he was paying the price.

Chapter 20

Pibrac South of France, September 2006 Alice's Birthday

She didn't think that a sky so blue could exist. She had seen many skies and this was the bluest by far. She shielded her eyes with her hand and the sun blazed over his shoulder. He bent slightly at the knees and brought his face closer to her, she saw his lightly tanned face and her eagle eye noted the stubble around his chin; he was handsome; she would give him that, in a sort of rugged way. Who was he? And what was he saying to her? She could see that he was trying very hard to speak slowly and was really stretching his mouth to make the word shapes, but she couldn't understand.

She turned to her son, offering up her puzzled look, "What is he saying?"

Her son laughed and explained. "This is our landlord Mum, he was saying how nice to meet you and wishing you a Happy Birthday... but he has forgotten you don't speak French, but he is really trying to make you understand."

She smiled at him and nodded, he took her hand and kissed it and then he was waving to her and moved away from the patio table and was talking with her son and his wife.

"How kind," she thought, " how nice of him to try and make the effort." She was genuinely touched. She watched him talking, waving his arms, gesticulating with his hands, she noticed his Gallic shrug, the confident way he exhaled his cigarette smoke. She thought about all the other words and languages that existed and she had not even been able to hear her own.

When he had gone, she asked after his name.

"Eric" they said, "But it is pronounced like this" and it had been written down. EREEK. She tried it out and they gave her thumbs up. She had just spoken French!

It was very hot for the end of September and it was so good to feel the warm sun on her face, she could feel it warming her bones. It felt good. Looking around the garden that seemed like a vast park, she once again shielded her eyes as the sun bounced on the blue swimming pool, making sparks of light dance on its surface. There were trees here that belonged in an English forest, tall oaks with acorns that had already fallen, trees that belonged in an English orchard, apples and cherries and nut trees; walnuts and hazelnuts and then there were the trees that would most definitely not belong in an English garden. Here were spiky palms and strange trees that she was told were called pine parasols looking like upside down umbrellas, here were vines that had been promising with fruit, but evidently had not born much. Here also were exotic looking plants with pink, white and crimson flowers, looking like orchids. Yesterday she had marvelled at squirrels with dark brown almost black coats, dashing through the branches of the nut trees and now she witnessed lizards basking on the stone terrace or scuttling away into the wall behind the pool.

As a small girl, she had never dreamt that one day she would come to her son`s home in France, she could never believe that she would fly on an aeroplane. Yesterday she had asked to go to the sea and so they took her. She had stood on the sand and gazed at the turquoise Mediterranean Sea. Albeit she would have loved to go for a paddle, but it was good that the beach had wooden walk ways leading to the water`s edge and with her little three wheeled walker, she had made it. Later sitting eating ice cream she allowed herself to feel young again and the smile in the photo said it all.

Yesterday they had asked her what she thought the most important invention was that she had seen developed in her lifetime. She supposed that they had imagined she would reply…. Space rockets, aircraft, the motor car…. She had replied, "The washing machine"

Today she continued writing in her velvet purple notebook that her daughter in law had given her. It seemed there were lots of stories that Alice had told them over the years, things that were crystal clear in her mind; but she was being urged to write them all down. So she sat and opened up the book again and wrote slowly, beautifully in her exquisite handwriting. She needed to rest her hand from time to time as her wrist ached, but she was determined to bring her writing into the present day.

"93" she thought about that, "how could she have got to be 93?"

She felt so much younger, except for her protesting body and the humiliation of needing help with intimate matters. Yesterday after her shower, her daughter had massaged her hands and feet and had hugged her so tight and she thought that when she had been wrapped in the large white towel, she had felt the love and seen the tears. For a brief moment it was a memory of her mother. She had never hated her, only questioned her actions, tried to understand and in writing she had discovered a woman who was struggling and who had executed a very harsh, tough love, but love it was.

Alice closed her eyes, wondering about the next chapter, her next big adventure. She hoped for sounds as well as sight, but for now she just wanted to stay in the warmth of the sun forever.

Epilogue

I first met Alice when I started dating her son. I found her fascinating and frustrating in equal measures, this wonderful woman who didn`t seem to let anything phase her. I was perhaps a thorn in her side as I was not the Catholic bride she had hoped for her son, perhaps I was also stirring up her status quo. She and her husband loved watching television, he had tried unsuccessfully to persuade her to have a television with subtitles---- she couldn`t see the need, I asked her to come and baby sit with me and she watched one of her favourite detective films with--- subtitles----result!

Alice and Joe were active members of The Bristol Deaf Centre and Alice was a member of the Bristol Deaf Catholic Church.

She still loved to go blackberry picking and still came home with a jam of blood and juice on her arms well into her late seventies--- She loved dancing, indoor bowls, trampolining, badminton----oh and she learnt to swim eventually---- when she was in her early eighties!!

Born in 1913, she saw many changes in her life and it is somewhat poignant that on the day her dear husband died, before he was taken to hospital, he had watched the disastrous launch and subsequent explosion of the Challenger space Shuttle. We once talked about all that had come to pass in her lifetime, ----- aviation, manned flight, the automobile, the jet engine, space craft, landing on the moon, manned space-station. She cited the washing machine and the vacuum cleaner as the most marvellous of inventions----here, here!!

When her beloved dog died, after a period of time we persuaded her to have a Hearing Dog for the Deaf---- Fidra was her beloved companion---- but maybe Alice needed a little more training---- but that`s another story!!

Alison Young

31 August 2017